HIRED GUN

They wait: six riders, rainwater streaming from their hat brims, their Saltillo blankets shielding their ready carbines, the Spur Barb riders are out to kill Dan Bryce, the gun-heavy stranger, hired by the Muleshoe outfit. Bryce will soon be lying dead in the mud, they figure. Bryce's loyalty has been bought, but there's also something there from his past and he has a personal score to settle of his own ... The Spur Barb-Muleshoe war will explode into deadly violence.

20.99

ARTHUR LYNN

◆

HIRED GUN

Complete and Unabridged

LP
W
L989h

LINFORD
Leicester

First pu[blished in Brit]ain in 2001

Originally published in paperback as
Hired Gun by Chuck Adams

First Linford Edition
published 2010

The moral right of the author has been asserted

British Library CIP Data

Lynn, Arthur.
    Hired gun.- -(Linford western library)
    1. Western stories.
    2. Large type books.
    I. Title II. Series. III. Adams, Chuck.
    823.9'14–dc22

    ISBN 978–1–44480–054–8

Published by
F. A. Thorpe (Publishing)
Anstey, Leicestershire

Set by Words & Graphics Ltd.
Anstey, Leicestershire
Printed and bound in Great Britain by
T. J. International Ltd., Padstow, Cornwall

This book is printed on acid-free paper

1

Dutch Kloot and what was left of his gang were smoking it out with the law in the town of Cholla, New Mexico, making its empty, sunbeaten street loud with crashing six-guns and foggy with drifting smoke. Kloot was holed up behind a crumbling adobe wall flanking Miguel Chavez's cantina. Shorty Haffner and Kid Billings were with him, lying in the dust, one at either end of the wall, firing across the street while Dutch was hunkered down halfway along the wall, shooting over the top.

Two Kloot men were lying dead outside the door of Chavez's drinking den, shot down as the gun-heavy outlaws made a wild dash out of the cantina in an attempt to get to their horses, hitched on the street as Marshal Bob Heaton and a couple of deputies had loosed a fusillade of slugs at

1

Chavez's back door and bellowed for Kloot and his men to come out peaceably. The gun-trap had worked tolerably well. Deputy Marshal Dan Bryce and half-a-dozen hastily sworn-in townsmen were waiting across the street, having already cut loose the hitched horses and sent them hazing.

When the ruckus started at the back of the cantina, the outlaws had rushed out of the front door. It was a grave mistake.

The Kloot gang, wanted for murder and bank robbery in Arizona, had made a stop to liquor up on their way to the Mexican border. They had figured Cholla to be a sleepy desert town with only rudimentary law-enforcement apparatus. They realized how wrong that figuring had been when they saw the black-clad Bryce and his men planted under the shading awnings across the street. They had been caught flat footed and recognized this as a time for pistol talk.

Two had slumped to the dust under

the slashing fire from Bryce and his companions, but Kloot, Haffner and Billings had taken a chance on a loping run for the safety of the nearby wall, Kid Billings suffering a bullet-bite as he scooted for cover.

Dan Bryce, 27 years of age, cold-eyed and with a reputation as a gunsharp gained elsewhere, was sprawled flat on the scuffed boardwalk across the rutted street, pegging shots at the wall while the deputies, shooting from the cover of empty packing-cases outside the general store at his back, slammed out a steady hail of lead.

'Throw up your guns, an' come out!' yelled Bryce at intervals. 'You can't win this game, Kloot!'

Dutch Kloot simply kept up his firing by way of an answer. Shorty Haffner and Kid Billings, whimpering with the pain of the slug lodged in his left shoulder, continued shooting.

'Be damned to you!' Kloot yelled through a tense lull in the exchange of slamming gunfire. 'We're smokin' it out!'

That was good enough for the law in the township of Cholla. They would keep shooting until Kloot's crew were either dead or they surrendered through lack of ammunition. The law hereabouts would have little scruple about shooting this bunch of hellions stone dead. Kloot's gang had blazed a trail of devilment across Arizona and had finally hared over the New Mexico line having pulled off a bank robbery in which a clerk had been killed and a woman customer who had run for the door screaming for the marshal had been brutally shot dead. Dutch Kloot knew that the Arizona Territorial Rangers had strung a tight line along the Arizona-Mexico border to intercept his kind of rannihan, so he and his gunmen had crossed into New Mexico in an attempt to haze over the territory's border with Mexico. But there would be no opportunity for the killers to cool their heels in mañana-land for a spell. Cholla, sun-pounded and fly-blown, had proved itself to have two smart lawmen in Marshal Bob Heaton and Deputy Dan Bryce.

Because of the woman they had shot in Arizona, the Kloot outfit was fair game for every conscientious badge-toter in the Southwest. Dutch knew that — and he knew well enough that this trigger-tripping bunch across the street were going to finish off his crew. It was ironic, he thought, that it should come here, in this measly desert-edge town, when the Kloot bunch had pulled clear of bigger townships with smart lawmen without suffering a scratch. If only he could get that lean, devil-be-damned badge-toter dressed in black, who looked so vulnerable, lying there on the opposite boardwalk, yet had an infuriating talent for ducking every bullet thrown at him.

It wouldn't take much to hit that *hombre*, Kloot thought, just a matter of edging a little higher over the wall to get his gunhand good and clear . . .

Dutch Kloot's last impressions of the world were the heat of the adobe wall against his free hand as he hoisted himself a little higher over the rim of the wall . . . the cursing and whimpering of Kid Billings as he blazed his Colt at the deputies . . . the constant *whang* and *ping* of bullets and the stink of gunsmoke on the hot air . . . the head of that black garbed deputy coming into line with the foresight of his .45, then a distantly and briefly glimpsed bloom of flame as the young deputy sprawled on the boardwalk fired first.

Kloot flopped over the wall like a bag of wet sand. Shorty Haffner saw him go down out of the tail of his eye. He turned a sweat-streaked, unbelieving face and said: 'Dutch? What happened?', regarded the still form of the outlaw leader then bellowed along the wall to Billings with a note of panic in his voice: 'They got Dutch, Kid! What do we do now? — They got Dutch!' Haffner, a sharp-featured little rannihan, had never been notably bright. He was the kind who had to be ordered about by a noisy bully such as Dutch

Kloot. With his leader gone, full realization that the Kloot outfit had been whittled down to just the kid and himself dawned upon him. Panic flared high in him.

'What do we do, Kid?'

Kid Billings offered no answer. He was busy with plans for his own salvation. He'd had enough of this pistol talk and the slug in his shoulder was giving him handfuls of hell. Nevertheless, the young outlaw had no desire to put up his gun and go out with his hands above his head to those devilishly determined Cholla deputies. He'd been mixed up in enough robbery and killing to be lulled into a long, long sleep by an application of hangrope medicine and he figured he was far too young to die.

As hostile bullets thumped into the dusty adobe of the wall, Kid Billings saw the gates of salvation beginning to inch open. There was a slight chance of getting clear of this fix and the kid saw it in the shape of his horse. When the deputies had sneaked the gang's mounts from the front of Chavez's place, they had hitched them well along the street, out of range of the gunplay that was sure to bust loose. But Billings' animal, a spirited little bronc, had contrived to yank its rein free of the rack. Scared by the fact that it was not under the guiding hand of a rider, as it had been when mixed up in previous shooting affairs, it danced white eyed with fear in the middle of the wide street while slugs snarled and revolvers exploded. The bronc was less than fifty yards away and Kid Billings figured he might just be able to make a dead run from behind the wall and reach it. Once he was in the saddle, he would stand a better chance of seeing his old age than if he remained holed up behind the wall with the panicky Haffner.

Kid Billings staked his life on an impulsive, spur-of-the-moment run. Before Haffner realized what was happening, the young outlaw was up and running.

'Kid! Where you goin'?' wailed the lonesome voice of Shorty Haffner as

Billings hoofed it, bent into a crouch, in the direction of the loose horse. But Kid Billings had put Shorty Haffner into his past. He was clear of the wall now and an open target for any one of the determined lawmen. There was a bewildered halt to the shooting as the deputies saw Billings hare from behind the wall.

Kid Billings turned his head in mid-flight. He saw the street and the hostile forces it contained at his back: the deputies crouching under cover on the far sidewalk, Marshal Bob Heaton and the men who had scared the Kloot outfit out of Chavez's cantina, squatting with ready sixguns outside the cantina having emerged from its front door when they had hazed the gang out. Those forces seemed too big and hostile to fight any more and the pain nagging at his shoulder was growing almost unbearable.

The kid outlaw pitched his gun down to the dust and stretched his legs towards the bronc. One of the hastily sworn-in deputies behind Bryce, flushed with the high spirit of battle, roared: 'We've got this one, he's just askin' to be gunned!' He flourished his Winchester towards Kid Billings' back.

Dan Bryce squirmed his body around on the harsh boards of the plankwalk: 'No!' he thundered to the eager townsman. 'He's unarmed an' you can't shoot him in the back!'

The man dropped the threatening Winchester and watched the kid outlaw hastily mounting the bronc. Billings, bending low in the saddle, clutching his wounded shoulder, hightailed it for the desert beyond the town in a blossom of risen dust.

Shorty Haffner realized he was alone. He was the last of the bunch, standing alone in bullet-noisy uproar. Shorty was no genius, but he'd been loyal to the Kloot bunch while it lasted; the sight of Kid Billings turning his yellow back on the fight caused some depth of last ditch courage in him to be plumbed. In the grip of a crimson, indignant fury, he came up from behind the low wall, Colt in hand, his face turned to the fast disappearing horseman.

'You lousy, yellow skunk!' he bawled to the kid outlaw's dust-obscured form. 'Stand an' fight, you stinkin' snake!' Haffner's short form was fully exposed to the men across the street and Deputy Dan Bryce was slowly uncoiling from his prone position on the planks.

'Throw down your gun!' he commanded. 'Throw it down an' walk over here!'

As though he had suddenly become aware that the forces of the law were there, Shorty Haffner whirled about to face Bryce and his men. The sworn-in townsmen of Cholla had never before seen the like of the curiously dead face under Haffner's sombrero: a face which bore a white-toothed grin and which had glittering eyes yet which seemed almost that of a corpse. But Dan Bryce had seen that expression before — on the faces of men determined to gun it out against high and hopeless odds.

'*To hell with you!*' screeched Haffner. '*I'm willin' to take as many of you with me as I can!*' His gun exploded as his mouth closed on the sentence, but Bryce was on his feet, standing with his body canted forward slightly. He dodged to one side so that the bullet Haffner had triggered at him went astray by inches and he tripped his trigger with deadly accuracy, the blast of his gun swallowing the last echoes of the shot Haffner had fired.

Haffner, still with that mask of deadness pinned to his face, jack-knifed slowly. Then he fell forward into the hoof-mauled dust of the street with gunsmoke coiling around his slumped form.

Cholla came to life once more when the shooting stopped. The citizens had taken refuge in stores and houses as the gunplay had flared on the street; now, they emerged to slap Bryce and the deputies on the back and pump their hands. They had seen the end of a desperate bunch of killers: there was some cause for civic pride in knowing that Dutch Kloot and his rannihans had met their Nemesis at the hands of Cholla deputies led by Marshal Heaton and that young fire-eater Dan Bryce.

Bryce dusted the grit of the plank-walk from the front of his black shirt and pants and someone asked: 'Shouldn't we go after that *hombre* who rode off into the desert?'

'Let him hightail to Mexico. He might have learned a mighty big lesson here in Cholla,' said Marshal Bob Heaton, lighting his corncob pipe philosophically. 'I figure we should turn our attentions to buryin' what's left of the Kloot bunch in Angels' Acre an' let that kid have himself a ride to a more healthy climate.'

Bob Heaton was pushing sixty. He was a lanky, tough featured South-westerner with spiky longhorn moustache and a constant air of doing things the lazy way. It was a deceptive air, for Heaton was a fast man with a gun and the ghosts of dozens of troublemakers, as

13

well as those of the Dutch Kloot outfit, could testify that it was an evil portent for the lawless breed when Marshal Bob Heaton came out of his adobe office with his gun oiled up and his eye showing a certain glint.

After the arrangements for the burial of the dead outlaws were made, Heaton and Bryce strode along towards the Marshal's office together. As they neared it, a voice hailed Dan Bryce and he turned to see Fred Hawberry, the agent from the stage office, angling across the street waving a letter.

'I would have given it to you earlier, but the shooting started just as I stepped out of my office. I ducked back again — quick!' grinned Hawberry, handing the Deputy Marshal the buff envelope.

Dan Bryce thanked him mechanically and studied the envelope. It was addressed to him in a hand he did not recognise. Letters were a distinct rarity for him. He had no kin and could not think who would write to him.

He walked into the office with Heaton who planted himself in the chair behind a spur-scarred desk and chuckled: 'Sure was a one way fight, Dan. There wasn't a darned thing the rest of the boys and I needed to do once we'd scared that crew out of Chavez's place into yore arms. Them fellers in Arizona are certainly goin' to be plumb sore when they learn it was New Mexico lawmen that settled the Kloot bunch after all the elaborate measures they've been takin'.'

'Sure,' drawled Dan absently.

He was standing by the door, reading the letter. The sun spilled in through the open portals, putting bright sparks of light on Bryce's holstered six-gun and the cartridges in his shell-belt. His face was long and handsome in a dark, slightly brooding fashion, sun-seared and wind-etched by the elements so that he appeared to be older than his years. He read the letter with serious eyes, then read it over a second time.

Bob Heaton was puffing his pipe,

chuckling quietly to himself as he reflected on the way 'them fellers in Arizona', would react to the news that Dutch Kloot had been finished off by New Mexico lawmen.

His good humour faded as Dan Bryce said quietly: 'Bob, I'm handin' in my badge!'

Heaton stared at him blankly, pipe protruding from his weather-punished face. He suddenly exploded:

'Handin' in your badge! For gosh sakes, Dan, what're you talkin' about?'

'Quittin',' said Bryce. He waved the letter. 'Sorry, Bob. but it's somethin' I'm obliged to do.'

Bob Heaton stabbed his pipe-stem towards the letter.

'Is it some kind of trouble — family trouble or somethin'?'

'Not exactly. I have no family, as I told you before. My family was killed by Comanches in Texas when I was just a baby. The Indians took me off when they razed our shack, but Texas Rangers caught up with them an' rescued me.'

He paused reflectively then added: 'I might have been a Comanche brave today, but for those Rangers — anyway, it seems my destiny is tied up with Texas. That's where I'm headed — back to Texas. I once made a promise to a man in Texas after he did me a big favour. Now, I'm bound to keep that promise — provided you'll accept my resignation, of course.'

Bob Heaton shrugged. 'You have the right to hand in yore badge any time you think fit, Dan, but I'm sorry to see you do it. You've done a tolerable big amount for this town in the couple of years you've been here. Still, if this thing is somethin' in the way of a duty, good luck to you.'

'Thanks, Bob.'

They went across the street to the more respectable of the town's two eating houses to have supper together later that evening. Later still, they had a few parting drinks in Miguel Chavez's place.

Heaton made no bones about Bryce's decision to leave Cholla, but he was sorry to see him go. The tall, fire-eating deputy had done a fair sized chore towards bringing a healthy respect for law and order to this town which nudged the Mexican border and which was a likely stopover for hard cases riding the owlhoot trail, since he rode in a couple of years back with a reputation for having cleaned up a rustler bunch almost single-handed at a place called Hix Creek.

Even later, Dan Bryce rode out of Cholla in the desert air of mid-spring and with all his earthly possessions bounding behind the saddle of his dun bronc in his saddle-tramp's warsack.

2

The letter, which was folded in Dan Bryce's shirt pocket as he rode for Texas, had awakened a memory that had long slept within him. It was written in the same good copper-plate hand in which the envelope had been addressed, the hand of a man who knew how to handle a pen, for all there was a wobble to some of the letters which spoke of a hand growing old.

The missive read:

> Muleshoe Ranch,
> Llano Diablo,
> Texas.
> March 3rd, 1879.

'Dear Dan,
   I never thought I would ever have to take you up on the offer you made

when some of my boys and I got you out of that fix in Fannin City a few years back, but that's what I'm doing in writing to you now. You said at the time that you would be glad to help the Muleshoe outfit out any time it needed help.

'Since then, I heard a good deal about you, especially about your part in the Hix Creek affair. One of my hands was in New Mexico some months back and heard you were Deputy Marshal in Cholla, which is why I'm writing this to you.

'To come to the point, Dan. Muleshoe is in trouble and needs a fighting man. It's a job for a Texas man of your kind and it's a risky one, so I'm not asking you to do it simply because you once said you would be happy to help out Muleshoe. I'll pay you good money.

'If you can make it, we'll be happy to see you show up at the Muleshoe headquarters, but watch your step once you ride into the Llano Diablo ranges.

'We'll be looking out for you.

'Yours sincerely,
Jim Phillimore.'

Dan Bryce thought about the letter and the memory it revived almost to the exclusion of all other things as he made his first night's ride towards Texas. It was the memory of a night in Fannin City, a mushroom Texas trail-town. As he thought of it, Dan could hear the bellowing of the shifting herds as they were prodded along in a sea of longhorns through the town's single street. He remembered the Texas riders whooping and yipping the animals along on the way to the Chisholm Trail; men tough as old saddle-leather whose throats were choked with dust. They would bed the critters down for the night on the flats beyond the town, then they'd leave a handful of night-herders circling the herd and ride back to town to get their bellies against a bar.

Bryce was a 21-year-old kid, holding down his first job as a deputy marshal. He knew there'd be trouble when the riders got to hard drinking — and there was.

It started in a poky little bar when two drunken cowpunchers got to trading blows over the favour of a Mexican woman who would scarcely have been granted a second glance by either cowboy had they been cold sober. Young Bryce had tried to bring some peace on to the scene through his own unaided efforts, the marshal of Fannin City being an old-timer whose best years were over and who was falling down drunk that night.

Dan had stepped in amiably enough and tried to separate the brawling cowhands. He made the mistake of forgetting he was a mere kid, that he toted the badge of law which trail-drivers were prone to treat with contempt, that almost everyone in the saloon belonged to the same cattle outfit as the fighting wranglers and were of the loudly expressed opinion that he was a young upstart sticking his nose into a private fight. Pretty soon, the original fight was forgotten and Dan Bryce was in a fight of his own — against a mob of drunken punchers.

They sailed into the kid deputy without mercy before he had the remotest chance of drawing his six-shooter. Within seconds, the cow-wranglers had Bryce on the floor and were mauling him with their boots.

It was at that point where Jim Phillimore and six of his Muleshoe cowhands made an appearance. Phillimore, owner of the Muleshoe Ranch in the Llano Diablo country, was driving a herd to the Chisholm Trail, a herd which had not yet reached Fannin City. He had bedded the beef on the fringes of town for the night and was seeking a drink with his foreman and a company of riders.

The Muleshoe men strolled into the saloon just as the mob of drunken hands were getting set to kick the living daylights out of the kid deputy, a procedure which did not appeal to the Llano Diablo cowhands.

Following the lead of big Jim Phillimore, who went charging forward with his spiky beard prodding the air like the prow of a fighting ship, they surged into the fight and began pounding the drunken wranglers with their fists. The Llano Diablo men had the advantage of being sober and they settled the affair in five minutes flat.

Big Jim Phillimore hauled the half-dead Dan Bryce up to his feet, shoved the kid towards the bar and filled him with a double dose of whiskey. It was then that Dan made his promise to the owner of the Muleshoe.

'Any time I can help you out, just let me know and I'll come runnin', mister,' he gasped.

It wasn't much of a promise: just the gratitude of a kid with his hair in his eyes and blood on his face and the bruises and cuts of boots and spurs on every inch of his hide. Jim Phillimore had grinned good-naturedly.

'Sure, kid. Have another drink!' he'd said.

And it might have passed off at that. But Jim Phillimore of the Muleshoe outfit remembered the kid deputy's name. It was a name which was to become famous after that run-in with the rustler crew at Hix Creek. Now, Jim Phillimore obviously needed help to the extent that he was willing to recall that moment against the bar in the grubby saloon in Fannin City and ask the kid who'd become a reputation gunhand to come a-running.

And so, Dan Bryce was bound for Texas once more: the same Dan Bryce who had once been rescued by Muleshoe riders when it seemed certain that he would be kicked to a pulp — and yet not the same Dan Bryce. This was a kid who had been hardened and shaped into a first grade trigger-tripper in the years since that fracas in Fannin City. Bryce was plenty tough and his gunhand was mighty fast.

There were those in Texas who were going to learn about him soon enough.

★ ★ ★

Bryce made good going, pushing the bronc hard, making a couple of stops in towns with hotels and spending three nights sleeping under the stars. He came to the Llano Diablo ranges on a broiling hot afternoon, an afternoon too hot even for Texas.

Since it was still only spring, there was something sinister about this burst of heat which set the far horizons shimmering.

Llano Diablo — the Devil's Plains — the place was well named, thought Bryce as he rode a gently falling slope. The land spread out before him, good gramma grassland with occasional rises crowned with clumps of live-oak. It was the kind of land on which cattle could thrive into well fleshed beasts which would bring good prices.

Bryce traversed the rich grassland and eventually hit a trail snaking its sunbeaten length away to the shimmering horizon. He followed it, allowing the bronc to take its time until he reached a post standing at one side of the trail. On the post was nailed a muleshoe and a crudely fashioned arrow pointed dead ahead. This then, was the trail to the Muleshoe outfit's headquarters.

The trail wound through the grassland like a yellow snake and thin puffs of dust rose from its sun-dried surface as Bryce paced the bronc along. Abruptly, the land became broken. There were high, cactus-greened rocks rising on either side of the trail. Dan Bryce rode between these rearing walls absently, his thoughts concerned with why big Jim Phillimore had sent for him. Then, this saddle-reverie was broken by a sound. A tiny sound, one almost inaudible, but one telling enough to set a man of Dan Bryce's background on the alert: the slight ring of a spur on rock.

Someone was up there, in the rocks, over to the right.

Bryce canted his head quickly towards the sound, then he heard a second sound which was really two quick sounds blended into one — the jerking of a Winchester lever. Whoever was hidden up in those tumbled rocks was out to kill Dan Bryce and had telegraphed his intention with the rasp of the lever pumping a round into a repeating rifle.

Bryce was in action even on the second note of the two-note sound. He canted his body over quickly, at the same time thrusting forward so that his head was obscured from the direction of the warning sound by his horse's neck. As he moved, two things happened. The bellowing cough of a repeater slammed from the rock, its shell slashing through the hot air where the rider's head had been a moment before, whining off the opposing rock wall with a dwindling scream.

And Dan Bryce's Peacemaker Colt slithered out of leather with an eye-baffling drawing action in the same shot-shattered instant he moved his body in the saddle. The dun bronc, surprised by the din of the would-be bushwhacker's repeater, pranced high and the moment the whining screech of the shell's ricochet died away, Bryce swung his body upwards like an uncoiling spring.

He was thinking calmly. Thinking that the man holed up in the high rocks must be several kinds of fool. In a country of this size and from his roost up there in the cactus-climbed rock-walls, the man must have been able to see the rider approaching miles away. He had all the time in the world to cock the Winchester before Bryce was near enough to hear it, then kill Bryce almost leisurely as he entered the rock-guarded section of the trail. Instead, he had bungled it. He had waited almost to the last second before he cocked the repeater

— and telegraphed the impending ambush to the man on the bronc.

Now, as he swung up from his crouching position in saddle leather, Bryce was figuring that a man who was that kind of fool might be fool enough to make another move. Would he stick his nose out from behind wherever he was hiding up yonder to see what effect his shot had had?

He was precisely that kind of fool. Almost the instant Dan sat up to his full height in the saddle, a head, crowned with a black sombrero, emerged from behind a boulder up on the rider's right. Bryce reacted like lightning, slamming a shot at the inquisitive head with trigger-speed which had been the undoing of lawless rannihans from Hix Creek to Cholla and several points between.

There was a half-heard croak on the tail of the shot, Bryce saw the inquisitive head drop behind the rock which sheltered the gunman and there was a thin anti-climax of sound as the bushwhacker's dropped Winchester skittered down the boulders, coming to rest in a yucca clump almost at the base of the rock-wall.

Dan Bryce waited for some reaction. Maybe there were two of them up there, maybe the man was not dead but only wounded — maybe he had a six-gun as well as the Winchester which he had lost and maybe he would come out from behind that rock with the weapon spitting fire. Bryce was a good target now, sitting at full height in his saddle. He waited in that position, purposely. The six-gun in his hand dribbled smoke, the gunfighter's eyes raked the rocky terrain.

If there's anyone left to fight, he thought, let 'em come out and make their fight *pronto!*

There was no reaction to the shot which had dropped the bushwhacker. There was nothing but the pounding heat, the smell of dust and cactus and a slight, hot-as-hell West Texas breeze touching Bryce's face.

Very slowly, Dan Bryce came down from the saddle; with his Peacemaker still naked in his hand, he began to climb the rocks to the point where the bushwhacker had been holed up. The man was huddled behind the rock, dead. Bryce's bullet had taken him through the forehead and blood spouted from the ugly wound, splashing crimson on the hot rocks.

Bryce stretched out the corpse and considered it with a cold and clinical stare. The man was young, probably under thirty. He wore sun-faded range gear and had a Navy Colt holstered in his shell belt. His face was a slack-jawed grimace, touched with streaks of blood, and Bryce did not have to exercise much imagination to see what kind of face it had been when animated by life — the tough face of a fellow turned bad early in life. Bryce grunted. This kind of *hombre* was just destined to die by gunfire or the hempen necktie, he reflected. Why the tough looking kid should want to kill a stranger riding the trail to the Muleshoe outfit was something Bryce aimed to find out; meanwhile, he was grateful for the fact that his would-be killer had been tardy enough to cock the Winchester when he was in hearing distance.

Dan reflected on the warning Jim Phillimore had included in his letter: he'd told the man from Cholla to watch out for trouble once he reached the Llano Diablo ranges. Never had a word of warning been more justified.

The sound of a horse's snort took Bryce's attention to a point higher up the slope. He walked steadily upwards and found that the man who had tried to kill him had tethered his steed behind some high, slab-sided rocks. It was a smart bay, trapped out with the sort of saddle and leathers a man such as the one now lying dead would own: the worn gear of a saddle-tramp. The horse, however, was not a saddle-tramp's animal. It was strong and well cared for. There was a brand burned in its flanks: a Spur Rowel, sometimes called the Spur Barb.

So, the animal belonged to a ranch, a ranch called the Spur Rowel, or the Spur Barb. Therefore, unless this rannihan who had tried to bushwhack him on the rock-flanked trail had stolen the horse, he too belonged to the Spur Barb or Spur Rowel outfit.

'I wish you could talk, critter,' Dan said to the horse. 'There's a question or two I'd like you to answer. Since you can't, I'm takin' you in tow to the Muleshoe headquarters.'

Thus, when he came to the end of the snake trail, riding into the yard of the Muleshoe Ranch, the black-eyed man from New Mexico had a spare horse tethered behind his bronc.

3

The Muleshoe headquarters had the spaciousness suited to the centre of a big spread — and Bryce had been given to believe that Jim Phillimore's outfit was in the high, wide and handsome Texas tradition: a ranch carved from land Phillimore had taken from the Comanche Indians the hard way. But there was something not quite right about the place.

Bryce was in the middle of the ranch yard before he fully divined what was wrong: it was run down. The house and the barns were ambitious and had once been smart, but they were smart no more. Outbuildings lacked paint, corral rails were warped and sagging in the sun and the yard was animal-fouled and littered in a way that no self-respecting ranch yard should be. In this, the boom time of the Texas cattle days, Muleshoe was a weary outfit!

There was a lack of activity about the place. No wranglers moved around the yard and the customary horses that went with any ranch headquarters were not even in evidence.

A door on the gallery of the house opened and a man emerged, a big man with a slight stoop to his shoulders who came out into the sunlight gingerly. He was a man who was growing old and one in whom Dan Bryce had difficulty in seeing big Jim Phillimore. His spiky beard was streaked with grey and there were deep-etched wrinkles in his face which Dan had not seen there when the fighting Muleshoe crew saved him from the clutches of the drunken trail herders so few years ago. Phillimore walked slowly forward to the gallery steps, screwing his eyes against the blaze of the sun to stare at the mounted man halted in the yard. A jittery hand hovered close to a Colt .45 holstered at his belt. Somehow, Jim Phillimore reminded Dan of the letters which made up the missive he had received from this ranch: proud but wobbly.

He had not been prepared to see big Jim Phillimore looking like this, ageing, obviously burdened and whittled down into an old man in the course of a mere handful of years. When he found his voice, he said:

'Hello, Jim. I'm here in answer to your letter.'

Phillimore's hand fell slowly away from the Colt at his belt. Belated recognition showed in eyes that were not so good as they once had been.

'Hello, Dan! Mighty glad to see you — sorry about the suspicion. I thought at first you'd be one of the unwelcome kind of visitor, we have some of that kind around!'

Bryce jerked his head in the direction of the led horse at the rear of his mount. 'I met one — that's his cayuse. He tried to kill me an' I killed him first. You certainly had cause to warn me to watch my step once I rode into Llano Diablo, Jim.'

Jim Phillimore leaned on the gallery rail. 'There's trouble a-plenty hereabouts, Dan. That's why I took you up on that offer you once made. Wouldn't have bothered if there wasn't real need, believe me.'

Dan came down from the saddle, stepped up to the gallery after hitching his bronc and took Jim Phillimore's hand.

'You can call on me any time, Jim, after the way you an' those 'punchers of yours pulled me out of the claws of that mob back in Fannin City. Only happy I'm not makin' crow-meat out on the trail where that *hombre* tried to bushwhack me.'

'Where'd it happen?'

'Back yonder where the trail runs between high walls of rock. This feller was posted up in the rocks with a Winchester. He made the mistake of waitin' to cock the rifle until when I was within hearin' distance. I found his cayuse. It has a spur branded on it. What's it mean, Jim?'

Jim Phillimore ushered the new-comer into the open door of the house.

'Spur Barb,' he said as they went. 'That's the name of the outfit neighbourin' Muleshoe, an' damned bad neighbours they've turned out to be.' He indicated a hide-covered easy chair at one side of a big ornamental fireplace, whose mantel was decorated with wide spanned longhorns and a couple of Yankee forage caps taken as battle souvenirs by Phillimore in the days when he fought for the Confederate States in a devil-be-damned Texas cavalry regiment. The rancher sat in the companion to Bryce's chair at the far side of the fireplace. He spoke quickly and with a slight quaver in his voice, in the way of a man opening his heart to reveal things locked therein for a long time.

'I'm bein' squeezed, Dan. I'm bein' squeezed dry by my neighbour, the Spur Barb outfit. It's owned by Jeff Criswell. We've been neighbours a long time, but there's no point in pretendin' we were ever real friends. We worked together to clear this land of Comanches, sure, we rode together as Texas Rangers for a spell when there was some mighty tough customers prowlin' these ranges. But we were never particularly friendly towards each other. We tolerated each other — we had to, since our lands joined each other's. We co-operated at round-up time an' all that kind of thing, just about keepin' up the bare essentials of bein' neighbours, I guess.

'Then a couple of years back, I got sick. Couldn't turn the place the way I wanted to for almost a year. My foreman an' hands did their best, but none of 'em has a real cattle-business head, though they're all damned good wranglers. Laid out with a serious illness, the way I was, a lot of good business went by the board. I lost several contracts, includin' an important one to supply beef to the army. Things kind of went from bad to worse. By the time I was back on my feet an' as fit as I'll ever be again, I was in pretty low water financially as well as in pretty low water literally. We had a drought worse than any in Texas history — it was like livin' on the doorstep of hell with its doors wide open. My water supplies plumb dried up an' I lost a lot of stock. The round-up wasn't worth a plugged peso that Fall.'

The old rancher paused to produce cigars and matches from his vest pocket. They lit up and Jim Phillimore gazed silently at the drifting wreaths of smoke as though he saw the bitterness of the past year reflected in them. Dan Bryce knew what the Muleshoe outfit meant to this tough old Texan cut from the old rock. Bachelor Phillimore had nothing else in the whole wide world but this outfit he had whipped Comanches to build. It was his wife and family and whole reason for being alive. He'd set out to build a ranch when he rode back in Texas after Lee's surrender in '65 and he'd gone through hell, high water and Indian arrows to build it. Now, he saw it crumbling around him like dissolving wisps of cigar smoke.

'I made the big mistake of goin' to my neighbour, Jeff Criswell, for a loan, Dan,' he explained when he resumed the narrative. 'His place is better watered from the uplands than mine an' he managed to come out of the drought in much better shape than Muleshoe. The blasted old skin-flint made a deal with me, making me put up some of my best graze joinin' his land as security. I managed to pay some of the money back to him but he started to press for a settlement. Claimed he had a right to take that section of pasture but I argued I could pay him what I owed him if he'd only give me a little more time. He kept pushin' for a foreclosure, then he just upped an' grabbed the land.'

'Grabbed it?' echoed Dan Bryce. 'What do you mean by that?'

'I mean he put his crew out one night an fenced off my land, addin' it to his own. He put up a damned, stinkin' wire fence!'

Dan blew out a feather of smoke and asked slowly: 'You mean one of those new-fangled barbed wire fences?'

Phillimore nodded an affirmative.

'He's a cattleman an' he put up a barbed wire fence! He must be a snake, Jim, an' no mistake!'

The words 'barbed wire' were almost a profanity in any cowman's ears. Barbed wire, but recently invented, was the device of the nester, the settler, the farmer, the little-minded man who had no use for free range. But anything so cruelly restrictive as barbed wire had no place in the affairs of men of the open ranges. Texas men were used to riding wild and free on unfenced land, allowing their cattle to mingle across sprawling acres, each outfit cutting out its stock, marking and branding, in the round-up seasons.

Here was a case of a cattleman who had not only grabbed land, but fenced it — fenced it with the despised barbed wire. Such a man, in the opinion of Dan Bryce, and in the opinions of many of like calibre, was a snake.

Phillimore filled in more details for the man in black. 'Some of my boys resented the fence,' he told Dan. 'One day, there was a ruckus with Spur Barb men and my men shootin' at each other across the fence. Then, the thing began to build up. Old Criswell began takin' tough customers on his payroll: the lead-throwin' kind who'd do anythin' for money. Then, next I knew was that the more squeamish among my hands was askin' for their time an' ridin' off the place. Most of 'em was plumb honest. Said they could see this thing was goin' to build right up into a first-class range-war an' they were cowhands not gunthrowers; if they wanted to get killed they'd join the army an' fight Injuns, but they didn't stomach hot lead on cow wrangler pay. I can't say I blame 'em for feelin' that way. My old hands stuck with me. They're a pretty loyal bunch, been with me since the early days an' this outfit means as much to them as it does to me. The trouble with them is that they're cattlemen — an' damned good ones — but they ain't trigger-trippers an' not much match for the kind of gentry Jeff Criswell is packin' into his bunkhouse.'

Dan Bryce nodded. 'So you figured you'd avail yourself of at least one *hombre* with a gun-reputation an' sent for me?'

'Sure, Dan, I need a fightin' man badly. Time was when I could have walked across this range right on to Jeff Criswell's place an' shoved the biggest barn on his yard area down his throat.' The old timer shook his head sadly.

'There's no point in my kiddin' myself I could fight this thing out on my lonesome now. I just couldn't do it!'

'This bushwhacker who laid up for me back on the trail — is that the kind of tactic Criswell is usin'?' Dan asked.

'Sure. I haven't lost any of my remainin' men through bushwhackin' yet, but Spur Barb is keepin' a pretty close eye on my section of the Llano

Diablo ranges. There's one move I want to make an' I figure they want to stall it pretty badly. I got a new contract. Got to get fifteen hundred head of beef into Dodge before the 20th of next month. It means a whole lot to me, but Criswell would like to stop me gettin' the cattle there. I don't know how he found out about the contract, but he did somehow. I met him in Diablo Flat, the nearest town to this location, just a few days ago. He told me he'd keep a tight eye on my ranges an' prevent me from gettin' those beeves to Dodge City. He knows damn' well that there's big money in the contract for me an' he knows what I'll do when I get that kind of money — I'll use it for lawyers' fees to take our differences to court an' get this fence business sorted out legally. He's mighty scared by that prospect because he knows he'll lose his argument in any properly convened court in the land.'

Dan twirled the cigar in his fingers, watching spirals of smoke rise slowly.

'I don't believe that galoot with the Winchester was squattin' in those rocks just takin' a peck at anythin' that might happen on your lands, Jim,' he told Phillimore. 'I think he was waitin' there because he *knew* I'd be along.

'As I remember that point of the trail, he wasn't in a good position to see very far across the rangeland, but he was in an almost perfect position to pick off a man who came ridin' towards Muleshoe. The whole thing seemed to be just plumb premeditated — the fact that he took his horse up to the rocks with him, so a tethered animal anywhere around the trail wouldn't whinny when my bronc approached just adds to my suspicion.'

Big Jim Phillimore considered the point for a moment.

'Maybe there's somethin' in that, Dan, but the only way the Spur Barb outfit would know you were comin' along would be if Criswell somehow saw the letter I sent you. It was mailed in Diablo Flat by one of my own boys an' I'm pretty sure that none of my crew would breathe a word to Spur Barb that you were comin' to Muleshoe.'

'It's plumb suspicious,' Bryce opined. 'I'd like to take a look at Muleshoe outfit, an' its wranglers my own self when the time is ripe.'

'Time is ripe tonight, Dan,' said a deep voice from the door. 'Today happens to be the Muleshoe pay-day. Them rannihans usually go into Diablo Flat on pay night an' get through a few bottles of liquor.'

Bryce looked up to see a tall man in range garb standing in the doorway of the room. His lean features were burned to the colour of old mahogany by the West Texas sun and he had the angular but supple look of a cattle wrangler cut from the old Texas rock. He moved across to the man from New Mexico, extending a horny hand.

'Name of Charlie Manders, foreman of this place.' he offered. 'Maybe you don't remember me, but I remember

48

you from that ruckus in Fannin City. You sure filled out tolerably since those days!'

Dan took the foreman's hand. 'I remember you all right, Charlie. You're the one who hauled me up from the floor when I was kicked half to death and you put your fist into the face of a drunken wrangler who came at us with a bowie knife.'

'The same,' admitted Manders modestly. 'Sure is good to see you here. I guess the boss has told you all the details of the trouble we're facin'?'

'I did,' said Phillimore. 'How's the herd shapin', Charlie?'

'Mighty well, Jim. I just rode back to tell you we have most of the good stuff gathered an' penned out on the west meadows. We could gather the full herd by sundown tomorrow an' make a start for Dodge the followin' day — provided Spur Barb don't get any smart ideas about scatterin' the herd durin' the night to fool up our chances of fulfillin' the contract on time.'

'You figure they'll try a move like that?' Dan enquired.

'I wouldn't put a blamed thing past Criswell,' said Phillimore. 'He doesn't want to see me get that herd to Dodge an' that polecat will try darned hard to stop me.'

Bryce took a last thoughtful drag at the butt of the cigar, then flicked it into the empty fireplace.

'We'll move that herd whenever you're ready,' he said with a hard glint in his eyes. 'Furthermore, we'll get it to Dodge on time. But first, I'd like to deliver some of Spur Barb's property to its owners — one bay horse, to be precise. How about showin' me the way to Diablo Flat when the Spur Barb crew is likely to be drinkin' there this evenin', Charlie?'

'Sure,' agreed Charlie Manders with the tough grin of a fighting Texan cut from the old rock.

4

Bryce and Charlie Manders rode across the Muleshoe ranges in the warm dusk after a bunkhouse meal during which the newcomer was introduced to the faithful few of the Muleshoe wranglers who had remained with the outfit. Behind Bryce's bronc trotted the bay branded with the Spur Barb iron which Dan intended to return to the Spur Barb men who, Manders assured him, would even now be a-helling with their pockets full of pay in the township of Diablo Flat.

Dan Bryce had another reason for wishing to clap eyes on the pistol-packers whom Jeff Criswell had taken on his payroll. He wanted to take the measure of these gunslingers and see for himself how much of a danger the other side really presented.

'D'you figure this thing will blow up

into a regular range-war, Charlie?' he asked the Muleshoe foreman as they rode with the hot evening wind in their faces. 'Or is this Criswell *hombre* just puttin' up a show of bluster — not that the way that fellow with the Winchester acted looked much like bluster to me.'

'It ain't bluster, Dan. Criswell has packed his place with the kind of ruffians who would shoot in any direction provided they were well enough paid. Get that kind of crew in any one place for a short space of time an' there's just got to be an explosion — an' there'll be one around here for sure!'

'I'm intrigued as to how that would-be bushwhacker knew I was comin',' Dan mused. 'Jim claims that no one from Muleshoe would tell a soul from Spur Barb that I was on my way here, yet that *hombre* was holed up in the rocks well enough to suggest he'd been there for some time, waitin' for a specific rider to show up on the trail.'

Inwardly, he gnawed at the question

as the pair paced their animals over the darkening land. Then another thought struck him and this prompted another question:

'How were the arrangements for this beef transaction of Muleshoe's made, Charlie — by letter?'

'Yeah,' nodded Manders. 'Jim received a letter from Tom Vickers, a Chicago dealer he's done business with a few times. That was the first part of the deal. The second part was when Jim wrote to Vickers agreein' to have the herd at the Dodge City railhead by the agreed date to ship them to Chicago. So far as I know, there were only two letters exchanged.'

'How do you mail letters hereabouts?'

'Through the express office at Diablo Flat. Why?'

'A notion just came into my head. Jim Phillimore told me that Jeff Criswell somehow got to know about the agreement to herd the beef up the trail to Dodge. That was a matter arranged by letter, just as my arrival here was arranged by letter. That makes two items which were supposed to be confidential and safe in the hands of the US Mail, but which became known to Criswell. D'you suppose Criswell would have a friend at the express office who would be low enough to open mail passin' between Muleshoe an' people outside this country?'

Charlie Manders slapped the flat of his hand against his leg with a loud *thwack*.

'By thunder!' he exclaimed with the air of one to whom an important fact had suddenly been revealed. 'The agent at the express office is Ernie Walburg — a man who once rode for Criswell!'

They took the three animals down a slant in the land to give them a blow and water them at a creek which was running at a low level in the heat of this West Texas spring.

'I figure that might be a very significant point,' observed Dan thoughtfully. 'If Walburg steamed open Muleshoe's mail, that's how Criswell got to know about the beef deal and about Jim's proposal to take me on as a hired gun. Spur Barb must have planted a sentry up on those high rocks for days, just waitin' for me to show up. It seems almost a pity that their patience wasn't better rewarded.'

A further hour of riding brought them to Diablo Flat. It was now almost dark and the town was a clutter of timber and adobe structures scattered on an unsheltered tract of flat land, backed by the high, dark and empty sky. Lights made a random pattern of yellow and orange, visible far across the prairie, and the squeaky music of a fiddle and the unmelodious voices of cowhands on the spree issued from the township.

'Sounds like the Spur Barb wranglers are in there an' spendin' fit to bust,' commented Manders. 'The Double Ace is their usual drinkin' haunt. Old Jeff Criswell usually gets in there with 'em — the cantankerous old rattler!'

They rode at an easy pace along the broad street of the town. It was a place which lacked the veneer of civilisation in the way that all Texas cowtowns lacked such frills. Weather-ravaged clapboard warped beside sun-dried adobe. The plankwalks were uneven and scuffed and the surface of the street was of dusty, hard-packed earth which would be a morass of mud in winter.

The Double Ace was a shaky wooden structure midway down the street. Yellow lights bloomed from its fly-blown windows across the backs of the ten horses hitched outside — horses on which Bryce saw the Spur Barb brand as he drew near and dismounted.

Manders and the man in black looped their reins about the hitchrack, placing their animals some little distance from those of the Spur Barb riders, but Dan hitched the led horse among those from the Spur Barb. Together, they breasted the batwing doors and strode into the saloon.

The place was filled with a drunken

cacophony of sound, issuing from a select group of men leaning against a far corner of the bar. The man from New Mexico noticed one characteristic at once: these men had the gunfighter stamp all over them, but they were not cowhands!

Other men, manifestly not of the Spur Barb outfit, stood in ones and twos at various points of the bar. Most of them seemed intent on drinking their liquor as quickly as possible and getting out of the presence of the Spur Barb hard-cases while the going was good. Attention became riveted on the pair from Muleshoe the moment they entered the drinking establishment. A short, curiously screwed-up little man with a curving longhorn moustache adorning a face which was as seamed as an old apple and burned to the colour of a walnut, stood in the centre of the singing group. He watched the approaching pair with eyes as bright as a bird's. Dan Bryce knew who he was before Charlie Manders nudged him and muttered: 'That's Jeff Criswell.'

Bryce and Manders confronted Criswell and his cowhands. The drunken attempts at song stopped at once and hard eyes were fixed on the newcomers. Bryce noticed one face among the gun-packers — a face he knew well from shakily drawn portraits on reward dodgers he'd seen in his days as a Deputy Marshal. He appeared to disregard the face, but the sight of it stirred deep memories in him.

Dan jerked a thumb in the direction of the door.

'I brought back a horse belongin' to your outfit,' he told Criswell. 'The man who owned it is dead — you'll find him up in the rocks where you planted him to kill me, Criswell.'

There was a long silence in which Criswell and his hired gunmen simply stared at Dan Bryce and the Muleshoe foreman. When the owner of the Spur Barb spoke, his voice was as melodious as a creaking gate on a windy night:

'What the hell are you talkin' about, Mister?' he demanded.

Charlie Manders, holding a languid

pose with his thumbs hooked into his shell-belt, answered softly: 'You know well enough, Criswell. You planted a man with a Winchester up in the rocks on the Muleshoe trail. You probably had a regular guard up in those rocks for days.'

'Yeah, just a-watchin' that trail for the day I came along it,' put in Dan Bryce, with a slight smile playing at the corners of his lips. 'You figured I'd be comin' sooner or later because you had Jim Phillimore's mail tampered with at the express office.'

Criswell's eyes moved in a brief downward glance and Dan knew he had hit home with the accusation. He was aware of tough, border scum faces regarding him with bleak stares — and there was one face in particular which he watched with the tail of his eye: that of the ruffian whose features had adorned the dodgers.

'You talk nonsense, Mister,' bluffed Jeff Criswell. 'I didn't plant any man in the rocks!'

'You did an' he's up there now — dead as mutton,' Bryce said flatly. 'Your men can go up an' collect him tomorrow, or leave him for the buzzards, but if I find any Spur Barb rannihan on Muleshoe land after sundown tomorrow, I'll ventilate him.'

'You talk powerful big,' drawled the man from the reward posters.

'I can back anythin' I say any way you want to play it, neighbour,' said Dan quietly.

He scarcely looked at the man who had spoken and did not change his stance in the slightest degree. The man from the reward dodgers checked his enthusiasm and simply continued staring at the man in black.

Jeff Criswell pushed in a hasty word of caution: 'We ain't proddin' for no ruckus with Phillimore's hired gun — yet,' he told Dan tartly. 'We got things to do. You go back an' tell Jim Phillimore that I'm pushin' a herd out for Dodge first thing tomorrow mornin'.'

Charlie Manders stared at the rival rancher.

'What d'you mean by that?' he demanded.

Criswell voiced his answer as though relishing each word: 'I mean I aim to get there first with that quantity of beef Tom Vickers has ordered. He'll take my beef if I get to the railhead an' Muleshoe misses out.'

'What is the hidden implication of that remark?' asked Dan Bryce with studied precision.

Criswell's walnut face split into a sour grin. He'd had a certain amount of drink tonight and it had loosened his tongue. He was finding some tipsy pleasure in dropping hints whereas, had he been entirely sober, he would have been as silent as a clam. He teetered playfully back and forth on his heels and stated: 'Phillimore's herd might come to grief on the drive — get bogged down or somethin' — or maybe it won't even get started!'

Abruptly, Charlie Manders looked at Bryce and the man from New Mexico remembered how the foreman had raised the question of Spur Barb making a move to scatter Phillimore's herd before it had a chance to leave its home pastures for Dodge. There was a deal of weight in the clumsy hints of Jeff Criswell. He recalled, too, that none of these Spur Barb men were honest cowhands. These were the gunsharps Criswell had taken on his payroll. Where were the regular cowhands who would normally be whooping it up in pay-night fashion in the saloon?

The answer to that poser was as plain as day to him, and he knew it was plain to Charlie Manders: *they were out on Muleshoe land, fixing to scatter the carefully gathered herd!*

That was cowboys' work, not a gunfighter's chore, though the Spur Barb riders might have a couple of hard-cases with them to take care of the night-herders.

Bryce showed no emotion.

'Your horse is outside,' he told Criswell, 'an' don't send any of your rannihans into Muleshoe country after tomorrow's sundown.'

He paused, then acknowledged the presence of the man whose face was on the reward posters for the first time by turning and looking directly at him. This man was on the edge of a gunfight. Bryce knew that well and, with his gunslinger's intuition, knew that it would come to a slug-fight between the two of them some day.

'Don't you try pullin' your shootin' iron when I turn my back, neighbour, or this will turn into your funeral party,' he warned between clenched teeth.

Manders and he turned about and walked out of the saloon, leaving stony faces and a tension-edged silence behind them.

5

Manders and Bryce mounted their animals outside the Double Ace and yanked the horses' noses in the direction of the Muleshoe ranges.

'That was a broad enough hint Criswell made,' commented Manders flatly, 'let's take a look an' see if that herd is safe.'

'How many men does Criswell have riding for him?' Dan asked.

'About a dozen out-an'-out range-hands — those nine *hombres* in there with him are all hired guns,' the foreman answered. 'It ain't like Criswell's hands to be missin' from the bar on pay-night, that's what makes me figure his outfit really is up to devilment with our herd.'

'That's exactly what I thought, but Criswell ain't likely to take on men for gun wages then keep 'em standin' around a bar while his hands do dangerous work on someone else's range. Were there any of his gunmen missin'?'

'Yeah, three that I can think of. Two hard-cases an' a dangerous lookin' Mexican.'

'Just sufficient to take care of the handful of night herders we'll have circlin' that bedded herd, while skilled cowhands get down to the business of drivin' an' scatterin' the critters,' mused Dan. 'An' this is the night for it — not a glimmer of moon.' They left town and raked their animals with spurs to send them thumping for the Muleshoe lands at a smart clip.

'That galoot who talked out of turn in there, what do they call him in this country, Charlie?'

'Joe Smith, a pretty nasty proposition.'

'Joe Smith, eh? Well he's known to the law as Rufe Hogan, an' he used to be tied up with Pete Hiller's rustler outfit, which doesn't say much for Jeff Criswell's choice of material when he hires extra hands.'

'Pete Hiller's gang?' echoed Charlie. 'That crew is still runnin' loose somewhere, ain't it?'

'Yeah, they had a run in with the law somewhere in the Indian Territory, a couple got killed an' the outfit scattered an' lay low. Hogan was Hiller's second in command an' he's wanted badly, though Criswell may not know that. I figure Hogan knows that I know who he is an' he's lookin' for a chance to ventilate me. One or two of the rustler persuasion would like to do that on account of the way I mixed it with the Hix Creek rustler crew.'

They rode rapidly over the now dark rangeland. The night was hot and the sullen heat seemed to hold the threat of imminent danger. They thought their own thoughts for a time, then Manders enquired: 'Why d'you figure those galoots are stayin' in town? I'd have thought Jeff Criswell would have packed all his gunslingers on to Muleshoe land if he really was goin' to scatter our herd.'

'No, he's playin' it smart. He's probably out to establish an alibi just in case anyone comes along afterwards an' asks where he an' his wranglers were the night Phillimore's herd was jimmied. He can say they were drinkin' in the Double Ace — an' the average man's memory is such that he might look back an' remember seein' Criswell an' a bunch of fellers in the saloon, without noticin' the detail that the men were all his hired gunpackers an' not regular wranglers!'

'Sure, I see the point,' murmured Manders.

There was a distant explosion — the thin report of a gun echoing far across the ranges. Then only the ominous silence of the hot night.

'That came from Muleshoe's west meadow — where the trail-herd is penned!' yelled Manders.

The pair ducked their heads low and put their animals to streaking like pony express mounts over the nightshrouded range. There was no further sound of shooting from the west meadow, which had the effect of making the situation seem even more tense, as though a single shot had finalised everything and put the situation out of the reach of the two speeding riders.

In the darkness, they topped a rise from which the black land slanted away into mile upon mile of good cattle grass, lost now in the cloak of night. Even as they reached the high point, there was the angry snarl of a gun — then another and yet another. The shots were nearer now, slamming their sound up from the land which slanted away into the night. Down there lay the Muleshoe's west meadow and from that direction came the shots and an even more fearsome sound: the concentrated thump of running cattle!

'Damn 'em,' snarled Manders, as the pair sat on halted horses on the crest of the rise, heads tilted to catch the sound on the still air. 'They've set the herd to runnin'!'

'And probably shot the night-herders!' growled Dan Bryce. 'C'mon — let's move!'

They plunged their mounts down the rise, riding furiously into the sound of pounding hoofs. Over the thunder of running cattle there came the thin crack of shots — shots which the rival wranglers were using to panic the animals along. Bryce reflected that the sound of the yet unseen herd appeared to be moving eastwards. Possibly, there were badlands in that direction and the Spur Barb hands were pushing the herd that way to scatter it and give the Muleshoe men hours of hazardous work combing bad country for the strays, so the start for Dodge would be delayed to Criswell's advantage.

'What lies eastward?' yelled Dan as their stretched-out mounts covered the dark land.

'The breaks. Very bad country. Them hellions are pushin' the herd that way, for sure!'

Bryce listened for an instant to the drumming of hundreds of hoofs, estimating the speed and the line of travel of the running herd which surged along somewhere in the darkness. Over the torrent of sound came the raggedly spaced blasts of pistols, proof that there was a body of riders somewhere at the back of the herd, stampeding it with shots.

'Lead the way to those breaks, Charlie!' Dan bawled into the heat-charged night air. 'If we can head the cattle off, we might have a chance of turnin' 'em around an' driving 'em back!'

Manders yanked his rein and hauled his mount about. He knew that to head off a madly running herd was no easy proposition, especially on a dark night such as this, but if the rival hands succeeded in hazing the beasts into the wild country of the breaks, the Muleshoe men would have to spend many precious hours the following day in rounding them up. Furthermore, the nature of the breaks was ragged and snarled and more than one crazily speeding cow would break her legs if chased into that country.

Both men knew, as they streaked for the breaks, that there was a further danger: if they manoeuvred badly in the darkness and placed themselves in the path of the unseen sea of cattle, they and their horses would be ploughed down by the furiously speeding beef. They went through the night like demons loosed from the gates of hell. The pounding of the herd grew louder, the land beneath their horses abruptly became rough and broken.

'We're at the edge of the breaks!' yelled Charlie Manders. 'Look out for rocks ahead!'

There was a sudden change in the volume and the direction of the sound of the stampeding Muleshoe beef: it was louder and nearer — and behind the backs of Bryce and Manders.

Bryce turned, saw the hazy sea of

shadows made by hundreds of lunging, tossing heads, tipped by wide-spanned longhorns, which was now surging in their wake.

'We're *in front of the herd!*' he roared to Manders. 'Get the hell out of here — an' shoot as you go!'

The pair punished their horses with spurs, and drew their six-guns to fire into the air as they streaked ahead of the crazed herd. In the darkness, the leaders of the herd shied at the sound of the shots issuing from their front, but they continued charging along in the wake of the retreating riders.

More shots echoed out of the blackness as Bryce and Manders continued to urge their horses deeper into the broken land; Bryce emptied his Colt into the air, then turned his head, not daring to slacken the speed of his crazily racing steed. He yelled a triumphant whoop:

'They're turnin', Charlie! They're turnin' about!'

He hauled his bronc around and

charged back in the direction of the herd which was now well into the fringe of the breaks, but turning back on itself in a milling, bawling chaos of tossing horns, seen only as bobbing barbs in the blackness. Bryce whooped and yelled hoarsely and Charlie Manders came pounding in his wake, shooting the last rounds in his sixgun and screaming rebel yells to scare the broken-spirited animals back.

And the herd was turning back. The mad stampede had ceased and the animals were whirling about like a sea in which the tide had completely turned. They protested with lusty bawlings, but they turned before the yelling pair on horseback.

'By grab, if them blasted Spur Barb hellions were ridin' after this bunch, they'd better watch out for the critters runnin' back at 'em,' rasped Manders, his voice husked with yelling. 'I wouldn't shed one little tear if they got ploughed under for the dirty work they tried here!'

The animals were drifting back out of the breaks, their headlong rush having ceased. They surged about in a dispirited fashion, tired after the plunging run across the rangeland and obedient to the whooping of Bryce and Manders.

There came the drumming of hoofs over the sound of the shifting herd and a harsh voice demanded through the blackness: 'What the hell's goin' on here?'

Manders yelled above the din of the cattle: 'Don't shoot, Jim, it's Bryce an' me!'

Jim Phillimore shouted: 'That you, Charlie? Damn it, we almost fired on you — thought you were them damned Spur Barb snakes. What the hell have they been up to?'

Dan Bryce and Charlie Manders took their weary broncs back to the edge of the broken country. Jim Phillimore was there, mounted at the head of half-a-dozen Muleshoe riders.

'We met Criswell in town an' he was

drunk enough to make it pretty blasted plain that his hellions were about to scatter our trail-herd,' Dan told the rancher. 'We got here fast an' the Spur Barb *hombres* had already started the beef to runnin' for the breaks. We didn't see anythin' of 'em but we heard 'em shootin' to scare the cows.'

Big Jim Phillimore, a dark hump on a big horse, loosed a string of colourful opinions in reference to Criswell and his outfit. 'We didn't see 'em, either,' he growled. 'They must have run off in a westerly direction, back to Spur Barb land, once they got the herd a-shiftin'. We found two of my night herders dead, though. Another one has a slug in his shoulder an' there's four more with me right now. I was up at the house thinkin' about whether that Criswell rattler would make any attempt to snarl up the herd, then the next thing I knew was a shot soundin' from this direction. I called out the boys and we hustled over there. We didn't see anythin' of Criswell's crew, just the broken brush pen where the beef had been herded an' a couple of dead herders with another one hurt an' the others' flounderin' around in an attempt to find out what was goin' on in the darkness.' The old rancher paused for breath, then more lurid opinions of Spur Barb. 'That damned Criswell is goin' to pay for this night's work. We lost two men — even if the herd is safe — that's too big a score to go unsettled!'

Dan Bryce pulled his bronc closer to Phillimore's horse. He said quietly: 'Jim, Criswell is puttin' his own herd on the trail for Dodge first thing tomorrow — that's why he tried to jimmy this one. He claims he'll supply the beef Vickers needs because you'll never get yours to the railhead. He knows about your deal with Vickers, the same way he knew I was about to come into this country: your mail was intercepted at the express office.'

'The blasted, low-down scum!' hissed Phillimore. 'Murder, hired gunslicks, barbed wire fences, runnin' off another man's cattle, interference with the mail — there's nothin' that stinkin' sidewinder won't stop at. Well, he won't get his herd to Dodge before mine! He missed out on his attempt to scatter or cripple this herd an' every last head of this beef moves for Dodge *tonight!* First, we bury the two boys them hellions killed; we'll get even for their deaths later. That snake wants a war an' now he's got one!'

Phillimore turned in his saddle and bawled to the shadowy horsemen at his back: 'Six of you boys get back to headquarters an' load up a chuck wagon, pile another with blankets an' the rest of the gear we'll need, then lock up the house an' round up all the horses on the outfit an' be ready to move within two hours — the Mule-shoe outfit is goin' on the trail if its the last thing it ever does!'

6

Banners of West Texas dust rose into the dawn-flushed skies as the Muleshoe herd moved off the Llano Diablo ranges in a great, surging, horn-foamed wave, prodded by whooping riders, the chuck wagon and gear wagons coming behind it and a *remuda* of spare horses following up the vehicles. Old Jim Phillimore was riding between the herd and the chuck wagon, grim-faced in the swirling dust, the early light putting the seams of his bearded features into high relief.

The fight with Jeff Criswell's Spur Barb outfit, with the drastic affairs of the previous night, had somehow given the tough old rancher a stoical determination. Yesterday, he'd been a man sliding down the grade, giving way to self-pity and allowing his unscrupulous neighbour to walk all over him. But the drama which had been acted out on the Muleshoe ranges the night before had made him into Big Jim Phillimore again: and it was the old Jim Phillimore who was taking every man and horse he owned to shove fifteen hundred head of beef up the trail to Kansas before Criswell beat him to it.

Dan Bryce, riding next to Phillimore, his mouth and nose covered by his bandanna to keep them free of the choking dust, rejoiced inwardly at seeing the emergence of the Jim Phillimore he remembered from the hell-roaring night in Fannin City. The old rancher, only his eyes visible in the scant aperture between his dust-peppered bandanna and the brim of his pulled-down hat, was cursing roundly. He had cursed almost continuously since the outfit set the herd moving before the first crack of dawn.

'By grab, I wish I'd caught them Spur Barb rannihans before they got a chance to run off my land last night!' he rumbled. 'Two men dead an' another

79

with a slug in his shoulder! By thunder, this herd gets into Dodge before Criswell's if I have to walk barefoot behind every critter pushin' 'em there with my own bare hands! If I meet up with that Spur Barb crew on the trail — I'll shoot every mother's son my own personal self . . . '

Phillimore growled and snorted and alternated his lurid swearing with instructions bawled to the riders ahead. Red and gold light from the new-born sun danced and sparkled through the hazy clouds of dry dust; the constant grumbling and bawling of the cattle and the higher notes of lowing calves made a restless undertone to the hoarsely-intoned yells of the riders. The herd was moving reluctantly with the curiously plaintive protests of trail-herd animals which seemed to have some knowledge that they were leaving their home ranges and going far afield to their very deaths. It was moving under the dynamic power of a tough and deter-mined old hand at the rail driving game who was going to get this mass of heads and horns where he wanted it in time or die in the attempt.

Dodge was the destination, wild and wide-open Dodge City, clustered about the recently laid railroad track on flat Kansas plains. Dodge which grew on the frontier like a mushroom — and which would die as quickly when the cattle days were through. Dodge, where thirsty cattlemen caroused and brawled and ventilated each other with Sam Colt's gift to the expanding American nation. Dodge, where Muleshoe might settle its final score with Spur Barb — if the rival ranch factions did not clash on the trail to Kansas.

Spur Barb was very much on top of Dan Bryce's mind as he rode beside Phillimore on that early stage of the trip.

'D'you figure he really will take a herd to Dodge, Jim?'

'He will,' Phillimore responded. 'That polecat would do anythin' to spite me — the move he made last night was just a spit in the wind to what the old hellion is capable of.'

The old rancher allowed himself a dry chuckle. 'Said he was gettin' started first thing this mornin', did he? Well, we got started even earlier, so we hold the ace. I'd like to have seen Criswell's face when he met up with them fellers who were on our land last night an' learned that they didn't scatter my herd!'

Dan rode in a brooding silence, head bent against the floating fog of dust streaming in the wake of the herd. The memory of the face on the reward dodgers kept returning to him: 'Joe Smith' that galoot called himself here in Texas, but he was Rufe Hogan, once second in command to the dark-of-the-moon rustler Pete Hiller. Thoughts of Pete Hiller followed those of Hogan in the black clad rider's mind. Hiller was ruthless and cunning. He'd scoured the Indian Territory and the Kansas plains with his cattle stealing crew, made a tolerably good thing out of it — and notched up more than a dozen murders in doing so.

Then, after a furious running fight with the law, some of the rustler outfit were killed and Pete Hiller and others somehow managed to escape retribution and lie low in places unknown. Now, Rufe Hogan, one of the wanted Hiller bunch, had showed up in the Llano Diablo ranges under the name of Joe Smith. Bryce remembered that Hogan was rumoured to be very close to Hiller in the organization of cattle thieves, headed by the latter — that he was, in fact, a substantial portion of the brains of the outfit.

As he rode in the lee of the bawling trail-herd, Dan Bryce's thoughts turned constantly to the Hiller crew which had apparently broken up and vanished.

Jeff Criswell started his herd about six that morning. As he shoved his cattle, his wranglers and his hired trigger-tripper bunch across his home ranges, bound northward, he was in a far from friendly mood. Last night's effort to scatter the Muleshoe herd and cripple Phillimore's beef in the breaks had failed miserably. His wranglers and the three hired gunmen who rode with them had returned with a shamefaced story about how they had been hazed off in the dark just as soon as they had set the Muleshoe beef to moving, having exchanged shots with the night-herders. Young Ben Grimes, one of the wranglers, had asked for his time there and then. He said at least one of the Muleshoe night-herders had been shot dead by one of the hired pistol packers and, while he was not averse to running off another man's cattle when there was a range ruckus on, he drew the line at outright killing. Criswell had paid the youthful rider and told him to go to hell.

The news that Phillimore's herd was safe and that his neighbour would shove that herd up the trail to Dodge was an irksome thing to Jeff Criswell. He bawled his hands into completing the arrangements for the drive and rampaged around his headquarters issuing orders at every turn and corner.

Joe Smith and the hired hellions were, as usual, keeping some way apart from the rest of the Spur Barb men who were plain wranglers.

Smith was idly oiling his Colt amid the gathered gunslingers in the ranch yard when Criswell came thundering along.

'Load a wagon with ammunition,' ordered the rancher.

Smith, a doughy-faced individual with dull eyes which totally disguised the sharpness of his brain, was unused to accepting curt orders from a hustling rancher. He considered Criswell dully and went on cleaning his pistol.

'You figure there'll be work for us on this drive?' he asked languidly.

'There'll be work, all right,' growled Criswell. 'You know how determined Phillimore is to have that herd in Dodge by the 20th an' you know how damned determined I am that he won't.

You seen his pistol-packer, the *hombre* who is supposed to have cleaned up the Hix Creek outfit single-handed. With that galoot to back his play, Phillimore aims to make a fight of this.'

One of the hired gunmen made a noise of contempt.

'Bryce? Huh, he's only one man,' he scorned.

'Don't underestimate him,' warned Smith in a flat voice. 'That business about the Hix Creek rustler outfit ain't just a story — it's true. He really did clean up that bunch on his own — or almost. Bryce is a tough customer.'

'I figured you thought so in the Double Ace last night,' observed one of the hired gunhands.

Smith turned on the man sharply and glowered at him.

'What the hell d'you mean by that?' he demanded.

'Nothin',' said the other. 'Didn't mean nothin' at all.'

Smith grunted: 'Don't insinuate that I'm scared of Bryce. His time'll come an' you'll see whether I'm scared of him or not.' He went on cleaning his Colt mechanically, his mouth set in a sullen line and his eyes brooding.

Criswell yipped: 'C'mon, you *hombres*, look alive an' get that wagon loaded. What the blue blazes do you think I'm payin' you for?'

Smith, who had come to hold a position of authority over the hired gun crew and packed more weight around Spur Barb than the ranch's foreman by reason of his gun reputation, prodded the men into action.

'All right, you heard Mr Criswell, get that wagon loaded an' let's move. We've a lot to do!' he growled, shoving his Colt back into its holster. Criswell turned and strode off across the yard to give his attention to another scene of preparatory activity.

'Sure do have a lot to do,' murmured one of the gunhands. And he winked largely at Joe Smith, known in other regions as Rufe Hogan, Pete Hiller's henchman.

Smith, his pasty features reflecting a certain waggishness for once, winked back.

The Spur Barb herd began to move for Dodge at about six a.m.

The Muleshoe herd pushed northward, heading in its slow moving, noisy way for the crossing of the Colorado River, as the sun slanted west and slipped down the wide bowl of the sky. filling it with varied tones of red and purple. Close to sundown, still several miles short of the Colorado, the riders circled the herd to bed it for the night.

The chuck wagon and oddments of wagons carrying various equipment were halted, the *remuda* of horses picketed and the scented smoke of a campfire was sent spiralling into the darkening sky.

Big Jim Phillimore and his Muleshoe men gathered around the fire where Washington, the Muleshoe's negro cook, had a coffee pot boiling. The scant breeze brought the mournful melody of a night herding song, sung by the riders who circled the bedded herd; it was soothing to the animals, if not particularly musical to the human ear.

It was while the hands were gathered at the fire, listening to Jim Phillimore's observation that the first day had been a tolerably good one, but that he aimed to shove the herd hard the next day, that a rider angled over the West Texas emptiness. He was a young man, riding a bronc which bore the distinct marks of a saddle tramp's cayuse. His trappings were those of any wrangler who chased cows in the wide open ranges of this country and he rode with the seemingly idle slouch of any Texas puncher. Had there been anyone to observe him as he rode through the gathering dusk across the vast land, they might have noticed that he was a young man who seemed to have some kind of preoccupation — also that he was watching the dark ground for some sign.

His name was Ben Grimes. He was a

cowhand in his early twenties, no worse — and perhaps a shade better — than most cow wranglers. Once, he rode for Jeff Criswell's Spur Barb outfit, but now, he was out of a job.

Grimes struck a section of the land which bore the recent marks of the passage of many animals. He halted his horse, bent low in the saddle for an instant, then gave a grunt of satisfaction. This track, discovered at the edge of night, was the sign he had been searching for during most of the day. He followed it.

It led him at length to the winking campfire of the Muleshoe drovers and the distant lowing of the restless herd.

Grimes rode slowly down a slant in the land, heading for where the canvas arch of the chuck-wagon stood flame-painted by the fire. Shadowy men who squatted with coffee cups and smokes around the fire came alive to the plod of his animal and the jingle of trappings. They stood up, turned their backs to the fire and watched his approach wordlessly.

Traditionally, any lone rider was given hospitality at a cattle outfit's fire at trail herd or round-up times, but there was a deadly rivalry among the men of this country and the hands of the wranglers standing at the fire hovered close to holstered side-arms as Grimes approached.

The young rider came into the glow of the fire. The Muleshoe men recognized him at once, saw the Navy Colt he packed and wondered what brought a Criswell rider here. Each had the same answer in his mind: spying, sent here by Criswell to locate the Muleshoe herd and see how far it had reached on the long trail to Dodge.

Grimes came down from his saddle, nodded to the Muleshoe men and said: 'Ben Grimes.'

Old Jim Phillimore, his bearded face splashed with the flickering colours of the fire, said curtly: 'We know you. A Spur Barb rider. What d'you want here?'

Grimes considered the hard eyes of the rancher and saw bleak hostility there. It was there, too, in the eyes of the Muleshoe foreman, Charlie Manders, in those of that black-garbed hired gun, Bryce, and the other Muleshoe wranglers standing at the fire. Funny thing, mused a portion of the young cowhand's mind unconnected with his main stream of thought, he'd got into Jeff Criswell's way of thinking about Phillimore. He'd imagined him to be a broken old man whose best days were over. Standing at this fire, right now, though, he looked tough as hell: a fighter who'd give no quarter.

Grimes shrugged his shoulders.

'Used to be a Spur Barb rider, Mr Phillimore, but I quit,' he said quietly. He nodded towards the coffee pot simmering on the fire. 'Any coffee left? Ain't had a drink in a whole day of ridin'.'

'Rustle him up some coffee an' give him what's left of the grub, Wash,' called Phillimore to the cook. 'What's it to us if you quit Criswell's outfit?' the rancher asked Grimes.

'Thought you might take on an extra hand,' answered the newcomer.

'A man out of *their* camp!' snorted Jim Phillimore, jerking the brim of his hat towards the night-cloaked horizon. 'Think I'm a greenhorn or somethin', Grimes?'

Manders, Bryce and the rest of the Muleshoe wranglers were watching Grimes with that same hostile glare. He knew what was in their minds. The same thing that was in Jim Phillimore's.

'Now, don't get me wrong, Mr Phillimore,' he said. 'I'm not spyin' for Criswell. I quit after that caper Spur Barb pulled on your land last night — after those herders of yours were killed.'

The fire put bright needles of light in Jim Phillimore's eyes.

'How were you involved in that business?' he asked with a dangerous edge to his voice. 'Were you one of the *hombres* who was on my land?'

'I was, but I didn't murder those herders — I didn't approve of it. I'm as bad as the next guy, an' just as reckless, an' there was a certain amount of devilment in hazin' your herd, but I didn't know outright, bloodthirsty murder was fixed for last night, or I wouldn't have gone on to your land — I'm a cowman, not a damned butcher!' There was a strong note of indignation in the youngster's voice. Dan Bryce, considering Grimes carefully from the shadows, thought the ex-Spur Barb rider's sentiments were genuine. He was a youngster who'd gone along on the cattle scaring caper for the devil-be-damned fun of it, but murder had been committed and the kid found no fun in that.

As Grimes took coffee and a plate of steaming food from Washington and settled himself on a flat stone beside the fire, Jim Phillimore asked: 'You mean that killin' was sort of premeditated? You mean Criswell ordered it?'

'I wouldn't say Criswell ordered it, but it was done by the kind of gun-packin' *hombre* that he's crammed on to his ranch an' that's slowly takin' over the place without him seemin' to notice. Three of them galoots went with a bunch of us who were straight-out cowhands by way of protection as we whooped up the herd an' scattered it. We were prepared for your night-herders to shoot at us, but the night was dark an' we figured we stood the best chance. What we didn't know was that two of those gunsharps — their names were Jones an' Britling — were out for some fun of their own. I tell you, Mr Phillimore, they killed your herders for plain, wicked fun. They went out of their way to do it when there was no need. One of the herders was only wounded, I guess, he rode off pretty quick, but Jones an' Britling killed the others for sure.'

Ben Grimes paused to sip his coffee.

'That was the score,' stated Phillimore. 'One wounded — an' two stone dead.'

Grimes nodded. 'It was the cold-blooded way them hellions went out to shoot themselves some night-herders, an' the way they laughed about it when we rode clear of your ranges that didn't set easy on me. I done a few things in my time, but I never was involved in murder before. I got to thinkin' Spur Barb was gettin' to be no place for a feller with my conscience, so I decided to quit an' asked for my time as soon as I got back to the ranch.'

'Now you want to ride for Mule-shoe?' asked Charlie Manders, touching a sliver of burning wood to his cigarette. There was still a hint of suspicion in the foreman's voice.

'Got to ride for someone,' replied Grimes. 'At first, I thought of movin' clear out of this country an' makin' a fresh start. Then, I got to thinkin' that Muleshoe was gettin' a plumb dirty deal from Spur Barb an' I'd like to help get your herd to Dodge before that bunch of beef that Criswell an' his crowd are pushin' there.'

'It could come to fightin' — an' probably will — d'you want to fight against your old bunkhouse partners?' asked Jim Phillimore.

'Not against my old *amigos*, no. Most of 'em are just plain ropin' an' ridin' men, but those damned gunsharps that Criswell put on the payroll are a different proposition. Those hellions are up to somethin' pretty deep, if you ask me, an' they're slowly takin' over the place. I only noticed it for the first time yesterday, it happened so darned gradual. That hellion Joe Smith is just edgin' himself into authority an' squeezin' Jeff Criswell out. It was after the shootin' of the night-herders that I decided I'd quit before I found myself workin' for Smith's outlaw bunch instead of Criswell.'

He munched the remainder of his food in silence, washed it down with the last of the coffee and added, musingly: 'Them gun-wage ruffians are up to somethin' for sure. Always gatherin' in quiet corners an' talkin' among themselves, takin' good care that no out-an'-out cowhand hears what they're sayin' — sort of plottin' is the only way I can put it.'

Bryce, a black clad ghost-shape with his back to the fire, asked: 'You say Criswell didn't order any shootin' of night-herders?'

'No. He just said we were to scatter the herd Muleshoe had gathered for the trail. Shootin' up the night-herders was just the way them blamed gun-slingers figured on havin' some fun.'

Dan Bryce cast his mind back to the meeting with Jeff Criswell in the Double Ace Saloon. He remembered that the owner of the Spur Barb outfit had denied setting a sentry up on the high rocks as a means of disposing of Bryce. Maybe he hadn't, but possibly 'Joe Smith', whom Bryce knew to be Rufe Hogan, had such power among the gunpackers on the Spur Barb spread, that he had planted the rifleman there.

It came to Bryce that Spur Barb might have an evil spirit working within its holdings in the form of 'Joe Smith'. This feud between the two ranches had started in a small enough way — as all such feuds started — but Jeff Criswell had imported the worst kind of outlaw to push his end of the fight for fancy wages. Could be, those men, under the evil leadership of 'Smith', were playing their own deep game.

The man from New Mexico played around with the thought as he rolled himself a fresh smoke. Maybe old Criswell hadn't posted the young fellow with the Winchester up there beside the trail to pick him off as he headed for Muleshoe but maybe 'Smith', late of Pete Hiller's rustler outfit had. 'Smith', playing his own deep game, could have good reason to fear the lawman who scattered the Hix Creek rustler bunch and, if Criswell had caught a tiger by the tail when he took on the crew of gunpackers, 'Smith' might be bossing this game more than even Criswell realized.

'I'd give a powerful lot to know exactly what's brewin' among them Spur Barb hellions,' said Dan Bryce to himself. *'And a powerful lot to jimmy their plans!'*

Out loud, he asked: 'What plans has Spur Barb to get their beef to Dodge before ours?'

'They'll push hard,' Grimes told him. 'I heard Criswell layin' out orders before I pulled out. He said he aimed to shove hard an' drive 'em through the night if need be. Said he'd shove towards the Colorado by way of the Palo Blanco country, he reckons it's tougher, but quicker.'

'Palo Blanco!' snorted Phillimore. 'That's tough country, all right. There's darn little grazin' for a herd of beef.'

'He says they can graze a-plenty once they've crossed the Colorado — but he aims to cross before you do.'

'He'll do it by grab,' grunted Jim Phillimore. 'Palo Blanco may be tough country an' hard on the animals, but a determined bunch of drovers *can* make good time to the Colorado goin' that way.'

'They also got to go through Mariposa Pass, that way,' mused Charlie Manders, a far away look in his eyes.

'A narrow pass where it's mighty hard to drive critters. An' they won't be there yet if they started out with the first light this mornin'.'

'What're you gettin' at?' asked Ben Grimes. Charlie Manders turned to him sharply. 'What's it to you what I'm gettin' at?' he flung at the man who had ridden for Spur Barb.

'Leave him be,' said Jim Phillimore. 'He's ridin' with us. I'm satisfied he's genuine an' he can be mighty useful to us, knowin' Criswell an' the Spur Barb crew the way he does.'

'In that case, I was thinkin' that, if my memory serves me right, Mariposa Pass has steep sides to it with plenty of boulders lyin' around 'em. A parcel of riders who were really determined could get from here to there tonight, shove some of them boulders down to dam up the pass an' make it plumb impossible for the Spur Barb critters to be driven through there.' The Muleshoe foreman blew a feather of cigarette smoke into the spiralling smoke of the campfire and watched the effect of his words on his hearers.

Dan Bryce grinned in the fireglow.

'Rememberin' the dirty trick Spur Barb pulled last night,' he murmured. 'I'd say one dirty move deserved another. How about you, Jim?'

Phillimore sprang to his feet, showing once more the old rejuvenation of spirit that this cattle-drive and race against his rival had worked in him.

'Don't need to ask me for an opinion,' he rumbled. 'Charlie, round up some of the boys who're in the mood for more ridin'. I'm goin' over to the *remuda* to haul out fresh horses. Damned if I ain't comin' on this caper myself!'

7

Mariposa Pass, a narrow channel of trail between high slopes, lay silent under a sky in which a thin wafer of moon offered brief moments of light filtering through scudding leaden clouds. The day had been hot, but those clouds held a threat which was unusual this deep into spring in this vicinity of Texas: rain.

The party of Muleshoe riders went cautiously through the night, angling up one of the slopes flanking the pass after riding at a fast lick from their trail camp. There were six of them: Jim Phillimore, Bryce, Manders, two Muleshoe men named Kelsey and Halligan and the newcomer from the Spur Barb outfit, Ben Grimes.

Up on the slope, they found a scattering of huge, rounded boulders, enough to block the narrow pass below if they rolled them down, a task which would take a good hour of steady labour. The Muleshoe men hobbled their horses on the heights, approached the first boulder and set to, a snorting, panting team, shoving the big rock until it was thrust from the position it had occupied for years and went rolling down the slope to thump into the middle of the trail. Phillimore and team grunted with satisfaction, caught their breath and moved to the next boulder. After a little more than an hour of shoving and sweating, they had blocked Mariposa Pass with a tangled clutter of huge boulders and the best drovers in the world would be unable to shove a herd of cattle through it.

Obeying natural cowboy instinct, they produced their makings as they squatted on the slope when the task was accomplished and Big Jim Phillimore shoved a blackened pipe into his mouth.

Dan Bryce was the first to hear a distant, tell-tale sound and he hissed a word of caution which stilled the fingers busily rolling cigarettes.

The sound came louder, constant and unmistakable: the bawling of hundreds of cattle on the hoof. Occasionally, the whooping voice of a rider pushing the cattle along was heard over the persistent lowing and grunting of the reluctantly moving herd.

'Spur Barb, by grab!' rumbled Halligan.

'Sure is,' Grimes murmured. 'Criswell meant what he said. He ain't restin' the beef anywhere, he's pushin' right through the night.'

'He ain't pushin' through Mariposa Pass,' Dan Bryce commented, shoving his unsmoked cigarette into a shirt pocket. 'We dammed the place up just in time. Better lie quiet and watch the fun.'

The Muleshoe men squatted close to their picketed horses, hardly discernible against the dark background of the slope. They waited as the fugitive moon slithered in and out of quickly speeding clouds. The threat of rain was strong in the wind which brought the increasing rumble of many hoofs, the grunting of massed cattle and the yipping of trail hands to their ears.

They slitted their eyes in the dim light, watching the far mouth of the pass. They saw the first of the cattle come into view far below, a dark, bobbing sea with horns making a scatter of white foam where the briefly appearing moon touched them. The pass became flooded by the slowly surging herd, plunging into the narrow channel between the high-rearing sides. Riders were bawling loud above the grunting of the animals, riding alongside the tight-packed herd and shoving persistent strays back where they belonged in the mainstream of the moving beef.

To the watching men, it seemed an eternity before the Spur Barb beef struck the scatter of boulders blocking the pass. When it did, there was a tumultuous surge of reaction down in the dark stream of horn-tipped heads, like a river turning its stream back on itself. The bellowing of the animals became bewildered and furious: the voice of a man, hoarse and profane, was raised high.

'*The blasted pass is blocked! Quit pushin' 'em through! Haze 'em back! Get 'em back, quick!*'

A frenzied chaos of sound, human and animal, was sent up from the living things surging around on the floor of Mariposa Pass. The voice of Jed Criswell was heard distinctly for a brief moment. He was swearing hard, yelling that the pass had been deliberately blocked only recently.

Far below the Muleshoe men, a furiously moving drama was being acted out with Spur Barb riders plunging in and out of the stream of beef, trying to turn it back to the entrance of the pass. Those riders were faced with a chore which would last a good part of this night. It would weary men and cattle and, if the Spur Barb trail crew still intended to go through Mariposa Pass to meet the Colorado, they would have to clear it of boulders by further hard work. If they altered their route at this stage of the trek, they were faced with going by way of a long detour.

Jim Phillimore considered the frantic, noisy business going on below.

'Good enough treatment for a bunch that'd run another man's beef into broken country an' shoot up his night-herders,' he commented wryly. 'Let's mount up an' leave 'em to it.'

The Muleshoe men climbed into their saddles at which point the moon slithered out from behind a bank of cloud. It showed up the party of six riders as they rimmed the top of the rise to make their retreat. From below, an excited voice screamed above the din of the struggling Spur Barb herd: '*Look up there! It's them Muleshoe stinkers, for sure! They blocked the pass!*'

Someone pegged a revolver shot up at the Muleshoe riders and Jeff

Criswell's voice screeched on the last echoing note of the blast: '*Quit that, you damn fool! D'you want to scare this beef worse than it is? D'you want us all tramped into the dirt?*'

Phillimore and his companions began to drop over the far hump of the rise. The last they heard of Spur Barb's dilemma was the angry voice of Criswell, rasping above the cattle-sounds, '*You ain't heard the finish of this, Muleshoe! I'll get even with you!*'

The Muleshoe outfit was moving with the first touches of dawn the following day and it reached the Colorado River shortly after noon. There was the frantic business of shoving the cattle across the stream at a fording place where the level of the water was comparatively low yet high enough to give the wranglers a busy time plunging after strays and calves in difficulties.

They crossed safely and plodded for several miles beyond the northern bank of the river and came to the second night camp with darkness sifting down over the sprawling land.

The rain in the leaden clouds had continued to threaten all that day, but it held off. The cattlemen knew that it would come — and come in spades when it arrived. Gone now was the fierce beating of the sun which pounded at a man as he covered mile after mile in a cracked saddle.

All of Texas had been set for one of the Lone Star State's long, bone-dry springs which would blaze out into the full fury of a parched and sizzling summer. But the first signs had been wrong. For a whole day, there had been the threat of rain and there was even a cool edge to the wind as the Muleshoe herd was bedded and a camp fire lighted on this far side of the Colorado.

Phillimore's wranglers hunkered about the flames Texas fashion, glad of warmth this ominously chill night. They smoked and drank coffee. Their clothes, sodden in swimming the Colorado, had dried on them. Something of the chill of the water seemed to remain in their bones, sharpened by the keen-edged breeze. There was comfort in squatting close to the fire tonight. The Muleshoe wranglers who were not circling the bedded herd soaked up its warmth and mused on the manner in which its rival had been handed a setback the previous night.

Meanwhile, the Spur Barb outfit was striving to make up for the time lost in hauling the herd clear of Mariposa Pass and in the strenuous work of clearing the pass of boulders to allow the passage of the trailherd. Spur Barb men had put in a long and wearisome night driving half-crazed beef back out of the pass to a bedding ground. Then, wranglers and hired gunmen alike, they shoved and hauled at the boulders blocking the narrow pass to break down the barrier created by the Muleshoe party.

Tempers were frayed among the Spur Barb men that night and their bodies were fatigued by hard effort over and above a full day of pushing beef up the trail. Then they gathered the bedded herd and set it to moving once more.

Jeff Criswell, storming at his crew and venting his anger at the Muleshoe bunch on every calf that stepped out of the mainstream of the sluggishly moving herd, insisted that they shove up the trail through part of the night to make up for lost time. His herders complied grumblingly and it was only the distinct threat of mutiny among the men which induced the owner of the Spur Barb outfit to finally call a halt at the edge of dawn with the Colorado yet to he crossed.

Night-herders, heavy eyed with the sweating, straining effort they had put in that night, circled the newly settled herd crooning doleful songs. The fire spread its warmth over a wide area and dead-tired men lay in their blankets within its glowing compass, oblivious to the hiss of rich-sapped firewood and the gathering clouds spreading their threat of dirty weather across the vista of the night sky.

But there were men in the Spur Barb

trail camp who did not sleep that night. One was Jeff Criswell, wrapped in an old Saltillo blanket, sitting with his back to a tree some distance from the fire and smoking his corncob pipe in a manner far removed from the philosophical composure which usually goes with pipe-smoking. Criswell was in a fuming temper. Muleshoe had stolen a march on him at the very outset of this trail drive and the Spur Barb rancher could not shake off the matter easily.

Another Spur Barb man who was not asleep at that moment was Joe Smith — known to the more knowledgeable as Rufe Hogan, late of Pete Hiller's cattle-thieving outfit. Smith was squatting behind a knot of rocks, removed from the fire and Jeff Criswell by several yards. With him were two of Criswell's hired gunsharps, Jones and Britling, the same pair who had killed the Muleshoe night-herders before both trailherds left the Llano Diablo country. Smith was talking urgently and in a low tone, so that there was no danger of others at the camp overhearing what he had to say.

'Start out tonight an' ride as hard as you can,' he instructed the gunpackers. 'Angle a little west until after you cross the Red River, that way, you'll avoid meetin' up with the Muleshoe bunch. Once you cross the Red, hit a flat out lick through Indian Territory. Down by the Cimarron, there's a broken down town called Peak Crossing. That's where Pete an' the rest of the boys are holin' up. The place is more than half dead an' there was no law there last time I saw it. It's exactly the place for Pete to wait around an' gather him a new crew.

'When you get there, tell Pete there's two big herds comin' up through the Territory for Dodge. You can figure that the Spur Barb critters will be a good couple of days later than Muleshoe's thanks to the smart trick them galoots pulled on us today. Still, that's all to the good. Pete an' his boys will have time to get Muleshoe's herd shifted before he

114

jumps Spur Barb's.'

Smith fished for his makings in a shirt pocket, rolled a smoke slowly, shoved it into his mouth and searched the pockets of his jeans for lucifers.

'That Bryce feller ridin' with Muleshoe is a problem,' cautioned Britling. 'He settled the Hix Creek bunch. He's death on rustlers. Anyone thinkin' of jumpin' a couple of herds had best make sure he's out of the way first.'

'Yeah,' rumbled Smith, as though mention of Dan Bryce had touched a sore spot on his hide, 'I tried to get him put out of the way early in this game, but the damned hellion slithered out of what was comin' to him. He's too damned brainy for old Criswell an' his bunch. Wouldn't be surprised if he wasn't the brains behind that move to block up Mariposa Pass. With him around, pullin' moves like that, this blamed parcel of beef is never goin' to get into Indian Territory an' Pete Hiller an' the boys will be waitin' around in vain.' Smith struck a lucifer and touched the flame to his cigarette. 'I was figurin' on takin' that *hombre* pretty soon — an' there'll be no mistake this time. You fellers move off an' do your stuff.'

Jones and Britling nodded.

'See you later,' murmured Jones, a small man with a mean face.

'Yeah — in Indian Territory, when the Pete Hiller bunch has gathered itself two nice big, costly herds, an' both sides of the Phillimore-Criswell feud have forgotten their grudges, 'cause they'll all be stone dead,' grunted Smith with wry humour.

Jones and Britling grinned, unfolded their squatting bodies to standing positions and bowlegged off towards the tree where the evil-tempered Jeff Criswell huddled in his Saltillo blanket, smoking and brooding on dark thoughts. He looked up at the pair as they approached with clicking spurs.

'Mr Criswell — we're quittin'!' said Jones flatly.

Jeff Criswell blinked at him through

wreaths of smoke.

'What d'you mean, quittin'?' he rasped drily.

'Ridin' off,' said Jones. 'We got tired of your blamed cattle drive.'

'Yeah,' put in Britling. 'We don't like pork an' beans an' too many days ridin' on saddle-sores. We took up with your outfit to help you protect your land. That was all right, but now you got us shovin' cattle up the trail an' haulin' rocks out of blocked-up passes. We worked ourselves near dead back at Mariposa Pass.'

'Frightened of a spot of hard work. I[s] that what ails you?' demanded Cris[p] acidly.

'We figured we'd ride on,' [said] Jones with an air of finality[. . . .] ridin' on tonight.'

'Ride on and be d[amned,]' snorted the ranch[er. . . .'I've] known some of [. . . . . .] would cry off v[. . . . .] You were paid ju[. . . . . . .] but I owe you a co[. . . . . . .]

comin' this far with the herd.' He rummaged under the blanket which covered his slight body, found his wallet and pitched a scattering of greenbacks down at their feet. 'Take that an' go to hell — ridin' your own cayuses, not any of mine!' he stipulated.

Jones and Britling smiled audaciously, picked up the money and began to stow it away.

'Thanks, Mr Criswell. No hard feelin's,' said Britling. 'Good luck with the herd. Might meet up with you again before too long.'

For no reason that Jeff Criswell could account for, this remark prompted chuckles from the pair of gunslicks. The rancher pushed his pipe back into his mouth and snorted, little realizing as the two men walked away from him what the future held for him, his men and his trail-herd.

8

Dan Bryce did not know it as he moved north with the Muleshoe trail-herd, but something of his own past had entered upon this drive to Dodge City of the rival Texan herds.

At the time when he and the Muleshoe wranglers were taking their ease by the campfire after blocking Mariposa Pass, a man was coming to the end of a long and lonesome ride up beyond the Red River which divided Texas from Indian Territory, that tract of sprawling plains country which would one day become the state of Oklahoma. This man was youthful and he rode a jaded horse with a stiffness to his shoulders which suggested a recent wound.

His name was Kid Billings and he was the last survivor of Dutch Kloot's outlaw bunch which had met its fate in a small New Mexico town when it faced a party of citizen deputies led by a determined lawman in black. Billings had made his escape into Mexico and languished there only a few days until his wounded shoulder was well on the way to healing. Mexico was no place for a man who was as broke as Kid Billings but, while south of the Rio Grande, he had encountered Americans who had lately left their native land with prices on their heads who told a tale which sounded as sweet music to the young survivor of the Dutch Kloot crew.

It seemed that there was a strong rumour that the bunch of rustlers which had operated under the evil genius of Pete Hiller was slowly emerging from hiding and planning great things in the way of lawbreaking. Hiller and his bunch, he heard, were holing up in a half-forgotten town named Peak Crossing on the far Cimarron River. They were looking for talent and Kid Billings considered himself to be as talented as most in the lawless ways of robbery, be it robbery of banks or of cows.

Accordingly, he forked his horse and rode north once more, going by way of Texas, where he was scarcely known, and taking care to make a long detour. He avoided the well travelled cattle trail routes which would have the first herds of the year upon them, but he made good time. He punished his horse with travel, took little sleep and lived on meagre rations.

He reached Peak Crossing late at night, trail-gaunt, hungry and broke. Billings figured he was the right material for Pete Hiller, but he had yet to meet that arch rustler who had preyed with great success upon the cattle trails.

Peak Crossing was nothing special so far as townships went. Nobody was likely to vote the place into the position of State Capital if Indian Territory ever became elevated to the dignity of statehood, thought the kid outlaw as he rode into the darkened streets of decrepit shacks and warped stores.

The place had its start in a gold strike which held the country in a brief and crazy thrall for a few months until it petered out as fast as it started. One or two hopefuls held on to the business they had started in the newly sprung-up town, making a seasonable trade out of the few cattle-herds which passed that way with their thirsty and hungry drovers. Most of the town had given up hope, put up the shutters and moved on. Only one saloon remained open and it was there that Pete Hiller held court.

Billings located the place and gained entrance to the presence of Pete Hiller. Hiller was a big man, built like a huge gorilla, decked out in range garb which had some refined touches, such as boots of Spanish tooled leather and silver trappings at his belt. He was surrounded by a choice company of cow-thieves, all of whom were looking forward to fat pickings when the spring brought trail herds to Indian Territory.

Pete Hiller listened with interest to the youngster who said he had ridden with Dutch Kloot. He also listened with undisguised suspicion. Hiller was constantly on the look out for spies who might infiltrate his ranks. The celebrated Pinkerton detective agency was only one law outfit which was out to bring the Hiller rustler crew to justice and the cunning Hiller never took any chances.

He was a good judge of men and a short consideration of Kid Billings convinced him that the youngster was tough enough and mean enough to ride with his rustler bunch.

Hiller and Billings sat one at either side of a scarred table with a bottle of bourbon between them.

'They tell me Dutch Kloot's outfit got cleaned up somewhere in New Mexico,' said the rustler chief.

Billings nodded. 'Yeah, I was the only one to get clear, but I had a slug in my shoulder an' had to hole up down in Mexico for a spell.'

Hiller passed a hand over his rough-stubbled chin thoughtfully.

'I'm always suspicious when a man is the only one to get clear after a mix-up with the law,' he grunted, his dark and dangerous eyes considering the newcomer carefully. 'You didn't rat on your *amigos* in any way did you, Billings?'

Billings thought it prudent to conceal the details of how he took his chance on catching a stray horse and riding for it when he and the last of his companions faced the guns of the deputy of Cholla and that town's armed citizenry. He shook his head vigorously. 'I didn't rat on anyone. I was just lucky enough to wriggle out of a hole with all my skin on. Afterwards, down in Mexico, I learned that the damned deputy who led the outfit that smoked it out with us was Bryce, the *hombre* who is supposed to have settled the Hix Creek bunch.'

Hiller drew his thick lips into a whistle.

'Well, it was Bryce, was it? The great Bryce about whom everyone has heard!

124

Is he as good as the stories say? Does he look like the sort of *hombre* who really could clean up a rustler crew on his own?'

'He's tough an' a hell of a man for shootin',' Billings conceded. 'Never saw a man get down to pistol play the way he does. Just settles down an' starts shootin' as though they were payin' him a hundred bucks for every slug. Strange thing is, he makes every shot effective an' he just plumb unnerves you.'

'Wouldn't unnerve me none,' rumbled Hiller. 'I heard about his kind before — the stories kind of gather a hell of a lot of glamour. When you meet up with the guy face to face, there's darn little to him.'

'There's plenty to Dan Bryce,' replied Billings with a conviction underlined by the nagging of the yet imperfectly healed slug wound in his shoulder.

'I wouldn't say I'm scared off by stories of Bryce's kind,' Hiller said, 'but I wouldn't want anyone with his ambition prowlin' around this territory right now. I got a very smart set-up all worked out to skim the best of the cream off this year's cattle-drive season. Pretty soon, I expect news that will put the new Pete Hiller bunch into action — an' there'll be some fat pickin's for all of us.'

Although Pete Hiller did not know it, the cattle stealing crew which he had formed about himself was going to be in action in a very short time. And the youngster who had just been accepted by the gang as its latest recruit brought trouble in his wake.

Trouble named Dan Bryce.

*　*　*

The first of the rain slanted in chill sheets across the vast land a couple of hours after the Spur Barb herd had crossed the Colorado River. It had threatened for a long time and now it had come in good earnest. This was still Texas and the rain had Texas-sized

126

ambition. It was going to be a mighty big rain.

Its cold drops gusted into the faces of Jeff Criswell and his herders as they shoved the sodden cattle across land which slithered in muddy treachery under their hoofs.

The men were at their business in a bent-headed and dejected fashion. They wore Saltillo blankets which had slits in the middle for their heads and which fell down to drape the whole of their bodies in the saddle. Bad temper was riding the surface of each of them as they rode herd with dripping hat-brims and rain-streaked faces.

Jeff Criswell came at the rear of the herd, plodding dejectedly beside Sid Clifford his foreman. The owner of Spur Barb was enfolded in his blanket, his hat pulled low and his empty pipe clenched between his teeth with the bowl reversed. He was in a silent, brooding, mood. He was remembering that Muleshoe had pulled a smart and humiliating trick in Mariposa Pass and that two of the hired gunnies had turned tail and wandered yonderly.

'*Just about the quality of these gun-sharps,*' thought Criswell in the dark regions of his mind. '*They can bluster around, but show 'em hard work like trail-drivin' an' they vamoose!*'

The herd made its struggling way northward. Criswell and his foreman rode in the lee of the Spur Barb chuck wagon, the rancher reflecting that he'd get this parcel of cattle to Dodge before Phillimore reached the railhead with his herd — even if every last man on his payroll quit and rode for the far yonder.

The thought was still in his mind when Joe Smith and almost the whole company of Criswell's hired gunmen came riding down the herd. Smith edged close to Jeff Criswell and rode knee-to-knee with the rancher.

'What d'you want?' demanded Criswell.

'Want to talk,' said Smith lazily.

'Want to quit, like Jones an' Britlin' now the weather's gone sour?' snorted Criswell scornfully.

Smith shrugged. 'Nope, want to talk about gettin' even with the Muleshoe bunch for that smart-alecky thing they pulled in Mariposa Pass.'

Criswell turned his wet face towards the leader of the hired gunslingers and began to pay attention. Sid Clifford simply stared at Smith and his companions in a stony fashion. The foreman had little time for the hired gunnies, he was an old hand who figured a cow-outfit should fight its wars without relying on border scum who were hired at better wages than range-hands. Sid was getting old and he'd been with Spur Barb since Criswell's early days as a rancher. Only a strong loyalty to his outfit — and the knowledge that he stood a slim chance of finding a job on another ranch had prevented Sid from riding off Spur Barb holdings when the hired gunslingers rode on.

'What're you figurin'?' asked Criswell.

'Gettin' rid of that hellion Bryce who's ridin' with Phillimore,' said Smith curtly. 'He's the one galoot who has brains enough to scotch our plans to get this herd to Dodge.' Smith, known in other regions as Rufe Hogan, was putting on a show of great loyalty to Spur Barb. 'That Bryce is one hellion with brains enough to louse up our plans,' he grumbled.

'That Bryce is one hellion who will shoot it out with you an' probably come off best from what I've heard of him,' commented Clifford with undisguised hostility.

Criswell and the gunmen ignored the foreman's verbal barb.

'What're you figurin'?' asked the rancher, addressing Smith.

'Figurin' that cow-drivin' ain't the work me an' the boys were cut out for — you got 'punchers to do that. Seems to me we should be goin' up ahead to fix that Bryce *hombre*; we don't want a repeat performance of the little game he and his friends played with us back at Mariposa Pass.'

Criswell turned his head and regarded the tough faces of the gun-hung gentry who rode behind Joe Smith. They were the hard faces of men bent on trouble, the faces of confirmed desperadoes intent on mischief.

'Seems to me,' purred Smith, 'we might stand a chance of fixin' Mister Bryce an' of doin' somethin' to halt the Muleshoe herd for a spell. That'd help us pull up some of the ground we lost at Mariposa Pass.'

One of the gunmen in the rainy background chuckled in anticipation.

'Somethin' like a small stampede might give them Muleshoe *hombres* somethin' to think about, Mr Criswell,' he suggested.

'I see what you mean,' murmured Jeff Criswell thoughtfully.

Sid Clifford, thinking his own thoughts, spat into the mud.

'How far do you reckon they've reached by now?' Smith asked.

Criswell did some mental calculation, reckoning distance and the time which had elapsed since his outfit last had any knowledge of the Muleshoe herd's whereabouts, which was at Mariposa Pass.

'Must have crossed the Brazos by this time,' he said. 'They'll be well on their way to the Red River and Injun territory.'

'Just a matter of locatin' their backtrail an' followin' 'em up,' observed Smith. 'Me an' the boys could do that easy enough — an' probably angle around in front of the herd an' the Muleshoe crew would find itself jumped before it knew where it was!'

'Yeah, sounds a tolerable good idea,' rumbled Criswell. 'Well, go ahead — get at it!'

'Knew you'd appreciate our point of view, Mr Criswell,' Smith grinned. 'See you up the trail in a few days' time.' He jerked his rein to send his bronc bounding forward, through the streaming rain, followed by the remainder of the hired gunsharps. The foreman of Spur Barb watched their blanket-wrapped figures go up past the struggling, bawling herd until the sheeting rain curtained them from view.

'Murder an' stampedin',' growled Sid Clifford. 'Damned if I know how low you can sink, Jeff — I should have lit out of your blamed ranch when that bunch showed up for your trigger wages.'

Criswell turned a sour, rain-punished face to Clifford.

'You can ride off now, if you don't approve of what's goin' on, Sid,' he stated acidly.

'I can't ride off an' leave a herd on the trail. I'm a cowman, Jeff — same as you used to be once, before you got to hirin' gunslingers — I'm bossin' this crew of wranglers an' we aim to get our beef to its destination. I'll quit at Dodge. You can pay me off there!'

'Now, wait a minute, Sid,' cautioned Criswell with remorse showing in his voice. 'Don't be so hasty. We been together a long time. We worked damned hard to build up Spur Barb.'

'Sure. There was a time when healthy competition was very enjoyable, but now it's come to a matter of fightin' over grudges, an' doin' it with hired guns!' complained Sid Clifford. 'I'd sooner have no part of that business.'

'Don't go gettin' all prissy, Sid. Have you forgotten who fired first? It was Muleshoe. They fired on our men over that fence.'

'They didn't kill nobody, they were just showin' there was plenty of disapproval on Muleshoe holdin's concernin' that fence. You shouldn't have fenced off disputed land, Jeff. I told you so at the time. No cowpuncher can stand the sight of a wire fence. This thing got deeper an' deeper an' now it's a matter of hired gunsharps layin' up for each other.'

'And we have the advantage there,' said Criswell with obvious satisfaction. 'We have a squad of gunslingers — Muleshoe has only one.'

Sid Clifford spat into the mud of the trail once more.

'It's damn little to be proud of,' he grumbled. 'You built this thing up into a matter of interferin' with mail an' settin' bushwhackers to layin' up for a man.'

'I didn't set no bushwhacker anywhere,' challenged Criswell.

'Bryce said you did that night at the Double Ace. Maybe that hellion Smith was responsible for that move, he's been actin' like he runs Spur Barb all along anyway. But you know damn' well that they've set out on a bushwhackin' spree now. I should have done what young Ben Grimes did when he saw what them gunnies of yours are capable of. I should have ridden off — an' I will do when I get paid off at Dodge!'

'Quit complainin',' growled Jeff Criswell. 'You're plumb forgettin' that Muleshoe made a dirty move against us at Mariposa Pass — an' it'll do so again unless we get one in first. You're gettin' to be almighty pious in your old age, Sid.'

'An' you're gettin' a damn sight wickeder in yours,' rumbled Clifford.

9

The rain continued to slash unmercifully at the herd which the Muleshoe riders were driving on the far side of the Brazos River. The long storm brawled over the land, the dripping cattle tramped through a morass of hoof-churned mud in a great glistening, horn-tipped flood.

Cowhands, drooped and draped in the sodden folds of Saltillo blankets, rode dejectedly through the slanting sheets of rain, keeping the animals moving with throaty yells and hoarse whoops. The Muleshoe herd was making good time, in spite of the fury of the rain. Phillimore, with droplets of rain streaming from his beard, was driving his men hard — he aimed to shove this bunch of beef-on-the-hoof much closer to the Red River, the dividing line between Texas and the

Indian Territory, before they were bedded for the night.

Dan Bryce rode hard with the 'punchers, making the best of the advantage gained with the blocking of Mariposa Pass. The animals, made miserable by the ceaseless downpour. trudged through the mud, bawling the usual protests of driven cattle. Bryce was draped in the usual Saltillo blanket. He pushed his bronc back and to along the line of cattle, riding hard on the occasional unco-operative stray which would attempt to wander out of the mainstream of the herd.

The herd moved. It moved in a sluggish, mud-bound fashion, but it moved under the constant, forceful pushing of dripping, bad-tempered Muleshoe herders — and it moved to Jim Phillimore's satisfaction.

The rain might have set the drovers' tempers on edge and dampened spirits in the Muleshoe outfit, but Jim Phillimore was as satisfied as any man soaked almost to the skin could be. This parcel of beef was moving as well as could be expected. Soon, night would fall, the herd would be bedded and the crossing of the Red River should be made some time in the middle of the next day.

Phillimore found a constant source of warmth in the memory of the way his men had halted the rival herd at Mariposa Pass. Criswell was going to have to drive his men and his beef to the last limits of their endurance if he hoped to have the Spur Barb herd make up for the time and ground lost back at the pass.

But, as Phillimore reflected on the strong lead which his plodding stream of cattle had established, he had no notion of the tightly packed bunch of riders who were at that moment thrusting through the storm, forcing their horses with the determination of men racing against time to accomplish a particular task. Smith and his gunnies had crossed the Brazos, they had shoved hard across the rain-pelted

Texan land and, with more luck than good planning, had struck the Muleshoe herd's back trail. That hoof-mauled and cow-fouled track which became lost in the constant flurries of wind-driven rain, brought a tight smile to the hard lips of Smith-Hogan.

'Just a matter of followin' this trail until we hit the herd,' he commented. 'When we hear the herd bawlin', we angle out of Muleshoe's backtrail pretty darned quick an' make a wide detour. We'll have to split the wind until we come out well in front of the Muleshoe bunch. Pick our spot right an' we'll fix Mister Dan Bryce for good.'

'An' no scatterin' the herd, eh, Rufe?' queried one of his companions, a gunnie not notably intelligent.

'I already told you that!' snapped Smith-Hogan angrily. 'That business about stampedin' the herd was just a line I was handin' Criswell to make him believe I'm interested in seein' Spur Barb make time to Dodge — which I ain't. Only thing I'm interested in is seein' Criswell's herd an' the Muleshoe herd bein' shoved right into Injun Territory where Pete an' the rest of the boys will be waitin' to grab both of 'em. Also, I want to see that blamed Bryce out of the way — he's too damned smart at bustin' up rustler crews!' Jouncing in his saddle, he glowered through the rain at the dim-witted rider. 'An' quit callin' me 'Rufe'!' he added as an after-thought. 'Don't even call me that out here away from Criswell's outfit, you're liable to forget yourself when Criswell an' his bunch are around. They ain't a bright crew, any of 'em, but the less they know the better.'

'D'you figure Phillimore will make an early camp tonight, Joe?' asked another gunslinger, laying strong emphasis on the assumed name.

'Naw, I figure he'll continue pushin' towards the Red as hard as he can to make up the lead Muleshoe gained back at Mariposa Pass. Phillimore is a stubborn old man an' I guess he'll keep goin' until weariness stops his cattle an' his men. That means we got to almost ride these horses dead if we're goin' to pull this thing off.'

This served as a good enough order for the bunch to quit talking and ride harder. With heads down in the sheeting rain and their soaking blankets flapping around them, Smith-Hogan and his gun-throwing crew speeded towards their mission which had everything to do with aiding Pete Hiller's projected grab of two trail herds and nothing to do with the ambitions of Jeff Criswell.

A good two hours of riding their near jaded animals with a punishing determination brought the crew of gunsharps within hearing distance of the moving herd.

Smith-Hogan listened with satisfaction to the grunting, complaining herd, sounding through the wind flurried rain.

'Straight ahead,' he murmured through tightly drawn lips. 'Angle off around that herd, you *hombres*. Ride fast an' make sure them Muleshoe fellers don't hear or see you. We'll find a spot up the trail where we can hole up for that hellion Bryce, an' remember — don't make any deliberate attempt to scatter the beef. Pete Hiller wants good beef when he jumps it, not stuff that's been half killed in a stampede. Some might start panickin' when we get to shootin', that's why we got to shoot first — an' make sure we get Bryce first — then we get the hell out of it!'

They angled off, like ghosts in the persistent rain, to jump the Muleshoe herd. It was the edge of night, the perfect time for an ambush.

Dan Bryce had lived for years as a gun-heavy drifter. There were signs he had learned to notice and read — and not all of them were visible signs. They were signs which spoke of trouble, however, signs which made a man who had lived as he had lived nudge his sixgun loose in his leather.

Such a sign showed in the cattle as

the Muleshoe crew shoved the herd northward through the monotonous rain and the gathering night. It was a nervousness, a tensed-up, scared quiver which seemed to shudder the whole of the way down the river of wet heads and jostling horns. Bryce was riding close to the head of the herd and he saw the sign and read its portent unfailingly. It spoke of danger ahead, the sort of danger which only a bunch of fractious cattle could sense trouble from; wild beasts, perhaps, but, maybe, trouble from hostile men . . .

Up ahead, they waited in the filthy weather, out to kill Dan Bryce.

Six riders waited in the rain, bunched together at the edge of the darkened trail. Water streamed from their pulled-down hat brims and their bodies were covered by heavy Saltillo blankets, traditional rain-wear on the Chisholm Trail. The blankets also served to keep the rain from the carbines they held ready for the man who would soon come up the trail.

Pretty soon, the waiting men figured, Dan Bryce, Muleshoe's hired gun and a danger to all rustlers, would be lying dead in the rain-pounded mud.

They waited patiently. Occasionally, one of their horses shifted its wearily drooped head as if to attempt to dodge the slamming bullets of rain. But the men in the saddles were as graven images. They were going to do this deed with Winchesters, it would be speedier and more accurate in this smother of rain.

'Remember, we don't want to drop Muleshoe riders all over the trail,' warned Smith-Hogan. 'We just want Bryce. You'll know him by the hat he was wearin' at the Double Ace that night if the rest of him is covered by a blanket — it's a flat-crowned black one.'

'What if them other Muleshoe galoots open fire?' asked one of the gunsharps.

'We don't give them a chance — we shoot the right man first time,' stated Smith.

They waited beside the muddy track, a cattle trail which had not been travelled by a large herd since the previous year. Up ahead of their horses' noses was a shoulder of tumbled rock and earth around which the trail wound. Pretty soon, now, the Muleshoe herd and, with it, Dan Bryce whom Rufe Hogan wanted out of the way, would come around that shoulder.

The half-dozen mounted men with Winchesters ready under their protective blankets waited . . . waited . . .

They heard the faintly defined noise of the approaching herd growing louder in the rainswept dusk; they heard the squelch of multitudinous hoofs, the constant yip of drovers, the nearing jingle of horse-trappings.

Under the protective blanket, Rufe Hogan's Winchester gave a sharp click as he pumped a round into the breech. Five similar clicks sounded in rapid succession from under the enveloping blankets covering the drooped, waiting forms of his companions.

Dan Bryce was up ahead of the herd, riding with a bunch of wranglers, when the warning ripple of fear surged through the cattle. Only a few yards ahead, the trail took a sweep around an outcropping shoulder, making a hazy bulk in the rainy night.

With the power of an electrical shock, it came to Bryce that danger, the unknown danger which was near enough to charge the herd with scared apprehension, lurked up ahead and around the looming shoulder of rocks. He touched spurs to his mount and lunged through the rain. Muleshoe cowhands, by now aware of the fear which the herd had registered, came in his backtrail, each grabbing for side-arms under his protective blanket.

Dan came around the shoulder: he saw the waiting men in one speeding flash as vivid as a flare of lightning. Six riders, planted on halted horses in the muddy lee of the outcropping. Their still attitudes told the man from New Mexico that this was a gun-trap. He bellowed a hoarse warning over his shoulder to the riders who came behind him with the first of the vast herd pressing hard on their heels. He pitched himself low in the saddle and grabbed for his gun as he yelled. But, even as he moved, he saw a white blast of fire slashing out from under the blanket of the middle rider and he felt a hot needle of flame tearing at the upper part of his left arm.

Half in the saddle and half out, Bryce fired from under the sodden Saltillo blanket in which he was draped. He saw one of the riders on the trail, mere yards ahead, topple out of leather as the bullet hit him. Muleshoe riders were suddenly prancing their horses to a halt beside Bryce, shots tearing in random confusion from beneath their blankets, clattering a loud tattoo across the wide, rainwrapped land.

The dimly seen bushwhackers were hazy ghosts, glimpsed through the sheets of rain. One was crumpled in the mud and the others were not attempting to answer the angry, ill-aimed shots of the Muleshoe men — they were yanking leather, turning their horses about. They were trying to make a getaway from a threat which they saw building up at the backs of the Muleshoe riders: the threat of stampeding cattle.

Those rapidly exchanged shots, blasted so close to a tight-packed parcel of beef already nervy because of the storm, had tripped the never reliable safety catch which held a moving herd in check. 'Don't give 'em any quick surprises' was the cowman's motto when his massed herd was showing restless signs. The sudden shots had given the Muleshoe herd one surprise too many — the very effect against which Smith-Hogan had warned his men had followed the brief blaze of shooting: they were running — and running with the terrible, unleashed fury which only hundreds of head of cattle possess.

Like water tearing out of a burst

dam, the Texas longhorns surged around the outcropping of rocks.

Dan Bryce, still ducking low in the saddle, face screwed in pain from the flesh wound in his arm, heard the approach of the terror rather than saw it. He was aware of the ground thundering under his horse as though some crazy giant were pounding a rapid tattoo on the land with both fists. In an incompletely grasped succession of pictures, he had a vision of the men who had waylaid the herd, plunging back through the curtains of rain, leaving one of their number dead in the path of the oncoming torrent of cattle; he glimpsed his companions fanning out wide, in headlong haste to drive their horses out of the path of the oncoming tide of beef; he heard the thin yells of the remainder of the Muleshoe drovers bawling rapid instructions to each other, miles away at his back, it seemed.

Bryce righted himself in the saddle with difficulty. He was in the first lunging wave of beef, caught in the spearhead of the stampede. He and his companions were isolated islands in a furious current of crazed longhorns. Clutching their saddle-horns with both hands, they held their legs drawn up high, clear of the madly jostling crest of horns. They fought to keep down their horses' panic. They fought to keep in the saddle and they fought to ride their animals clear of the stampede before the horns of the cattle slashed and speared them to death.

One stumble, in this headlong nightmare of charging animals pounding like a dark tide through the rain-lashed night, would bring horses and men down under the rapidly hammering hoofs to be mauled into the mud. And the mud was an added hazard. Riding in the ordinary way was difficult enough on a night like this when the elements had churned the Texas dust into a slithery morass of treachery. To steer a horse out of a press of stampeding longhorns under these conditions was an undertaking wherein a wrangler needed all the luck in the cards.

Bryce clutched his saddle-horn, cursing the hot pain of the ripped flesh of his injured arm, cursing the bushwhackers who had appeared on the trail and who had now hazed into the storm-cloaked night.

The world was filled with thunder and Bryce rode the horse down the onward tearing stream of loosed cattle, not urging the mount but allowing it to gallop along in the thick of the stampede, as though carried by the force of a tide. He had lost sight of the Muleshoe men who had been with him at the fore of the trail-herd now. They were isolated somewhere in the sea of horns, each fighting his own battle against the terror-on-the-hoof, using cowboy savvy to ride with the tide and edge his steed to the fringe of the stampede and, if luck was with him, ride clear.

Bryce plunged through the thundering night with resentment and fiery anger blazing in him. In that brief instant in which the bushwhackers had come so close to killing him, he had glimpsed a face. A face which told him all he needed to know about the attempt at murder on the night-cloaked trail.

As the muzzle-fire of the Winchester ripped the darkness, it cast a spark of light against the face of the man who had fired it. Even as he made his speedy downward lunge to clear himself from the path of the bullet, Bryce noted that face: the doughy, unemotional face of the man known at Spur Barb as Joe Smith, but whom Bryce knew to be Rufe Hogan, second-in-command to Pete Hiller, the rustler from Indian Territory.

Now, as he battled to ride his cattle-surrounded mount clear of the thundering herd, Bryce had a dozen dark thoughts marching through his mind. The pain of his bullet-ripped shoulder put an edge to his thoughts of vengeance.

'By the great horned toad, if I get out of this fix, I'll meet up with them Spur Barb hellions an' smoke this out man to man with every last one of 'em,' he told himself.

For that short-lived lick of light against the features of Rufe Hogan had told him that this was a Spur Barb move — another move similar to that of planting a man up in the rocks on the trail to Muleshoe headquarters after Criswell's confederate at the express office had tampered with the mail. Maybe it was a move to kill a few Muleshoe men, maybe a deliberate attempt to stampede the Muleshoe herd. If it was the latter, it had certainly been a success.

At all events, it was a Spur Barb move to get even for Muleshoe's triumph at Mariposa Pass. Bottling up cattle as the Muleshoe wranglers had done at the pass, was one thing, setting out with outright murder in mind was another, reflected Dan. This dim-trail bushwhack attempt, which had been successful in sending the torrent of Muleshoe cattle haring for the horizon, was sufficient proof that Jeff Criswell's outfit wanted a fight with no punches pulled — if ever such proof were required.

'*All right,*' growled Dan Bryce to himself. '*They'll get the kind of fight they want if I pull myself out of this ruckus with a whole skin!*'

Though he thought coldly and without panic, Bryce was physically in one of the most dangerous situations of his life. He and his mount were tearing along at a furious rate amid the ocean of horns with a storm of hoofs thundering under them. Rain lashed at the rider's face and there were breath-taking instants when his bronc lurched and it seemed that both horse and man must go to their deaths under the hammering surge of crazed cattle.

The blackness of the night seemed to have intensified and Bryce felt remote from the remainder of the Muleshoe crew. Somewhere in this mass of pitching, hastening longhorns were the men with whom he had been riding at the head of the herd but he could not see them. Perhaps, whispered an unbidden voice of fear, they had been unhorsed and ploughed down into the mud under the drumming hoofs. Somewhere, lost at his back, were the owner of Muleshoe and the remainder of the trail-herders, but Bryce had no notion of where they were. Once, before he had become isolated in this storm of running beasts, he had heard Phillimore and the wranglers bawling in an attempt to halt the stampede, but their voices had long since been drowned by the persistent drumming of the panicky cattle.

He crouched low in his saddle, without a notion as to where the horn-tipped tide which swept the bronc and him along was travelling. They were now far removed from the well-travelled cattle-trail along which beef had been moved for season after season; they were out in the emptiness of rain-washed land, plunging along in the teeth of the wind and the rain.

Abruptly, Dan Bryce became aware that the effect which he knew would occur if only he could stay alive long enough to see it was taking place in the running herd — the cattle were thinning. Where there had been tightly packed, horn-barbed heads, spaces were appearing. As a natural effect of running wild without the supervision of riders posted at strategic intervals along the herd, as when on the trail, the mass of cattle was widening its ranks. Weary beasts at the fringes of the stampede were dropping out and straying, gaps were widening between beast and beast. The stampede was breaking up. Pretty soon, it would stop because of sheer weariness and the herd would be scattered in isolated clumps of cattle across the land.

This was the effect for which Bryce had waited. It was easier for a rider to move in the midst of the cattle now. The racing animals were wearied and they were slowing down; very soon, they would be merely walking and Bryce would be able to ride between them and take his scared, horn-torn bronc out of the fringe of the herd.

He calculated his moment well, riding his bronc with expert control, slowing the frightened animal as the herd slowed and talking to it soothingly. He saw a gap between cows at one side, shoved the bronc through it; saw another and pushed the bronc again, always working towards the margin of the stream of cattle. Almost before he realized it, the weary animals had dropped their headlong rush to a mere walk. They were tired now and the uncanny, spellbinding quality of mass determination which seemed to grip and control them during the stampede was gone. Once more, they were stupid cows, ambling along and bawling like the lost things they were.

Bryce slowed the bronc to keep pace with the beef, then made his way out of the herd, riding through the thinned-out beasts until he was in the rain-slammed open. The bronc was a good cattle animal, bought from a man back in Cholla who had raised it on the ranges. It had not suffered greatly from its experience, though the lunging horns had inevitably torn some of its hide.

Dan rode through the blackness, back-tracking along the stream of the now walking herd, looking for Mule-shoe companions. He soon realized that he had been in only a small segment of the complete Muleshoe herd. Some-how, possibly by good riding tactics on the part of Phillimore and the rest of the trail-crew, who had been lost somewhere at his rear, the herd had been split. Possibly, he thought with satisfaction, Jim Phillimore and his wranglers had been able to discipline the greater part of the mass of beef, cutting loose this head-of-the-herd section, allowing it to run free and wear itself down to a walk.

He heard the jingle of horse trap-pings and, remembering Spur Barb's part in the dirty work of this night, dropped his right hand down to the gun holstered under his Saltillo blanket. The pain of the flesh wound in his left arm seemed to increase now that he had time to think about it and his anger increased accordingly.

Three mounted ghost-figures appeared in front of him in the gusting sheets of rain and his hand left the pistol holstered as a familiar voice called: 'That you, Dan?'

'Yeah. You all right?' he answered.

'Sure. We're all right an' Tom Couzzins is over on the other side of the beef, he's all right, too, but his cayuse is mighty cut up by horns. Can't find Mex Salinas, though, he seems to have plumb disappeared.'

Dan grunted and rode up to meet the riders. They were the men with whom he had travelled at the head of the herd. They were safe, but the news of Mex Salinas' disappearance was ominous.

'Did that *hombre* with the Winchester hit you?' asked one of the Muleshoe men.

159

'Nicked me in the arm, but it's nothin',' Bryce replied. 'We'd best round up this parcel of beef an' see if we can take 'em back to the main herd. Keep a look out for Mex.'

Wearily, they set to work in the darkness. Rounding up the loose cattle was not easy and several head were probably still ranging loose in the blackness, but they parcelled up a more or less orderly bunch and pushed it back across the land over which the stampede had run.

In the rain-torn blackness, they heard the lowing of the rest of the herd, obviously under control. Their smaller segment joined the big herd, flowing into it under the natural attraction of cattle for cattle and with a minimum of pushing.

Jim Phillimore, Charlie Manders and other Muleshoe men, wearied through hasty riding and desperate herd-stopping work, appeared out of the rain.

'You men safe?' growled Phillimore.

'Safe enough,' Bryce told him. 'But

160

we lost Mex Salinas.'

'We found Mex — what's left of him — back yonder,' said Jim Phillimore mechanically. 'He was trampled. We'll have to wait until mornin' before we bury him. I heard shots. Did them Spur Barb hellions start this?'

'They started it, all right, a bunch of Criswell's hired gunnies jumped us back where the trail took that twist around a hump of land,' Dan said flatly. 'They got clear away from us when the herd began to rush. They nicked me in the arm.'

The man from New Mexico spoke the words in a half-interested way, but the memory of Rufe Hogan was like a grinding, aching wound. He remembered the brief glimpse of the rustler's face in the flash of muzzle-fire from the Winchester; remembered how he had first spotted Hogan in the Double Ace, when he knew there would come a time in this feud when he would have to face Hogan and smoke it out with him.

Now the stampede which Hogan had

sparked off had resulted in the death of Mex Salinas, ploughed into the slippery dirt by a torrent of panicky cattle hoofs.

From this point on, Dan Bryce was prodding for Rufe Hogan. From this point on, he was going to even the score for Mex Salinas.

The Muleshoe men rode back to the chuck wagon where Washington prepared hot water and began to clean and dress the wound in Bryce's upper arm. Bryce noticed that the bullet-slash had the effect of stiffening his arm and fingers,

'Good thing it ain't my right hand,' he said meaningfully.

10

Jones and Britling came to Peak Crossing in the mounting, sultry heat of afternoon. Here, in the Cimarron River country of Indian Territory, there was the promise of summer — the dry and sun-pounded summer of this untamed land — hanging in the air almost like a threat. The long storm which had broken the dry Texas spring, away beyond the Canadian and the Red Rivers, had not touched Indian Territory.

The pair who had been dispatched from the Spur Barb trail-herd by Rufe Hogan had made good time in traversing the spiny, harshly folded land which spread its tawny length between the rivers. They found Peak Crossing more than half asleep. A semi-ghost town at the best of times, it seemed to have capitulated all signs of life to the threat of a long, sizzling summer.

A grimy Indian, huddled in a blanket and asleep in the door of a derelict store, gave a brief indication as to the whereabouts of the saloon where Pete Hiller spent his time after Britling had dismounted and awakened him with the toe of his boot. They entered the saloon, which was as run-down and used-up as everything else in Peak Crossing and were quite unprepared for the number of men to be found inside its peeled and crazily-hinged batwing doors.

Pete Hiller, with his usual show of elegant dress, was holding court — and what amounted to a small army of men, all very obvious hard-cases, was gathered about him.

Hiller did not speak as the two trail-wearied men entered with spurs dragging across the grimy floor, but there was a question in his brooding eyes as he considered Jones and Britling.

'Rufe sent us,' Britling said by way of introduction.

Hiller had a glass of good quality bourbon in his thick fingers. He raised it to his lips, finished the drink with one fell swig, placed the glass on the table in front of him and wiped the back of his hand across his mouth before he bothered to answer. Then he asked:

'So Rufe sent you. What's the word?'

'The word is that two big, fat herds are movin' this way, both of 'em headin' for Dodge more or less neck an' neck,' Britling said.

'Mighty good pickin's,' observed Jones.

Pete Hiller chuckled in a dry and totally humourless fashion. The rustler crew, recruited from some of the toughest bullet-throwing scum in many hundred miles, listened intently and bright eyed.

'Two herds!' exclaimed Hiller. 'Last time I heard from Rufe by our own peculiar postal service he was fixin' to steer Criswell's Spur Barb herd right into our lap by way of openin' the season. Whose is the second herd?'

'Criswell's neighbour, a feller called Phillimore of the Muleshoe outfit down in the Llano Diablo,' Jones said. 'He an' Criswell are in the middle of a feud an' they're each out to get to Dodge before the other.'

Pete Hiller chuckled again.

'Big Jim Phillimore! Used to be a well known personality where cowpunchin' was concerned. But he's old an' worn out by all the tales I hear,' the rustler chieftain rumbled. 'Ain't much of a threat from Phillimore, I figure. Sure, I know about the feud, that's why Rufe an' some other *hombres* took up with Criswell's outfit, 'cause he was payin' gun-wages. Criswell figured they were nothin' but true blue to him, but the fact of the matter is they were all set to steer his first trail-herd of the season right into the little set-up the new an' improved Pete Hiller gang has all ready for 'em. But I guess you know all that.'

'Sure, we know all that,' confirmed Britling. 'But there's one more thing you should know: Phillimore has Dan

Bryce ridin' with him. Rufe figures he'll fix Bryce, before the herds get into Injun Territory, but when we left Criswell's trail-crew, Bryce was still alive an' ridin' with Phillimore.'

'Dan Bryce,' Hiller growled. 'Dan Bryce, the galoot who is supposed to have cleaned up the Hix Creek bunch all on his lonesome!' He spat at the scuffed boardwork of the floor. 'All them damned legends about Bryce bein' hell on wheels when it comes to shootin' up rustler outfits don't strike me as bein' anythin' more than legends!'

There was a movement among the gathered rustler crew, a movement from a young rannihan who had lately joined Hiller's newly gathered brood of hard-cases, a young man who held one of his shoulders as though it had lately been injured.

'I wouldn't discount him that easy,' counselled the youngster. 'The Hix Creek outfit ain't all he jimmied: he also sewed up what was left of Dutch

Kloot's crew down in a no-account place in New Mexico. I was there — an' got a slug in me. He's hell on wheels, all right!' Something close to fear showed in Kid Billings' eyes.

It did not escape the notice of Pete Hiller.

He asked: 'You scared of Bryce, Kid? If you are, you can ride. I got a good, big crew built up here an' a right secret place to hide the beef until we blot the brands. I aim to pull in both those herds that're bound for Dodge pretty soon after they get over the Canadian an' it ain't goin' to be any place for a kid with no stomach for a fight.'

Billings was young, but tough and he'd had a pistol at his belt since his earliest teens. Nothing irked him so much as a jibe about his lack of years. A spark of temper flickered in his eyes.

'I ain't feared of Bryce,' he snapped angrily. Bravado prompted him to add: 'As a matter of fact, I'm lookin' forward to meetin' up with him again, so I can get even for Dutch Kloot an' the rest of the boys that hellion finished off.' He thought it prudent to conceal the facts of how he jumped on a stray horse, leaving Shorty Haffner to face Bryce and the Cholla citizenry that day in New Mexico. 'Yeah, I'm even lookin' forward to meetin' up with him again!' he emphasized, largely to convince no one but himself.

'Good thing you are, Kid,' stated Hiller levelly. 'You better have all your guts with you when you ride over the Canadian with this bunch, because there's goin' to be some fightin' before we get them two herds tucked away — an' we're ridin' right now!'

Within an hour, Hiller's army of rustlers was a-horse and riding south for the Canadian River country, intent on pulling in the biggest haul of stolen beef any rustler bunch had ever handled.

* * *

The Muleshoe trail-herd pushed hard across the vastness of north Texas.

Wranglers bawled and bullied the beef along through days that were, in contrast with the cold fury of the storm, oven hot and chokingly dry.

There was a mood of furious anger in the whole of the trail-crew, from Jim Phillimore, storming along on horse-back, his beard jutting forward like the prow of a fighting ship, to Washington, the negro cook, who went about his work of driving the chuck wagon, dishing up grub and washing crockery with silent and furious determination. This streak of fury showed in the way broncs were ridden along the mass of noisy cattle and in the way men talked snappily to each other and to the beef.

In its own way, Muleshoe was mourning Mex Salinas.

Mex had been a popular Muleshoe rider and there had been little enough left of him after the stampede. What did remain of the dead man had been given the most decent burial the Muleshoe trail-drovers could contrive in the welter of rain and the morass underfoot.

He had died as no square-shootin' cow wrangler deserved to die, declared the men of Muleshoe, and he had been killed by the trickery of Spur Barb and its hired gunslicks.

The Muleshoe wranglers burned for revenge and their blazing fury was expressed in the way they shoved the gathered beef north in a determined effort to reach Dodge City and fill the beef contract before their Spur Barb rivals. They took the minimum amount of rest, bedding the cattle early each night and starting them on the trail early each morning.

Muleshoe men rode the cattle hard, sweated, swore and kept their fighting energies pent-up for the big explosion they felt must come when they met up with Jeff Criswell and his Spur Barb crew.

Meanwhile, they aimed to see the contractor who waited for the herd supplied with his beef before Spur Barb reached Dodge and stole their market. To that end, they shoved the cattle in a way in which few of them had ever shoved cattle before.

Dan Bryce, riding with an improvised bandage around the bullet-bite in his arm, was in the swim with the wranglers, punching the cows with determined energy — but always thinking of that doughy face which had showed in the fleeting instant of the muzzle fire from a Winchester hidden under a Saltillo blanket. Rufe Hogan had sparked off that stampede. Rufe Hogan had caused the death of Mex Salinas.

The more Bryce considered these points, the more he saw Hogan as the evil spirit in the Spur Barb ranks. Accordingly, the conviction he had known that night in the Double Ace, before the Muleshoe herd left the Llano Diablo country, the conviction that he would have to kill Rufe Hogan, grew in him. Spur Barb had played a mighty dirty game when all the facts were considered. There was the matter of the intercepted mail; there was the bushwhacker planted in the high rocks on the Muleshoe trail, waiting for Bryce; there was the scattering of the Muleshoe cattle and the killing of the night herders on the eve of this trail-drive. Now, there was the final straw: the death of Mex Salinas under the feet of the madly running cattle.

Criswell's Spur Barb crew made good time after the night of the storm, largely because of the advantage it had gained over the Muleshoe men when they put in the irksome, time-wasting labour of rounding up cattle which had scattered every which way. The Spur Barb trail-herd crossed the Red River into Indian Territory on an afternoon when the sun was high and hot, beating mercilessly on men and beasts who had so lately been shivering under the onslaught of rain in the cold-edged spring storm.

Jeff Criswell took a large amount of satisfaction in seeing his hundreds of head go streaming across the narrow fording place on the Red while his mounted wranglers pranced their horses around in the water, hoarsely urging the cattle over the broad, sluggish ribbon of water to the far bank. Pretty soon, now, they would be in the open and sparsely settled midst of Indian Territory and, once the herd had traversed this region, Kansas and the booming railhead of Dodge City awaited it. The owner of the Spur Barb outfit was warmly confident that he now had the edge on the Muleshoe herders. His neighbour Phillimore and his herd would have to do a powerful amount of hard travelling if they were even going to catch up with the Spur Barb herd, he reckoned — thanks to that smart move Joe Smith and his gunsharps pulled the night they scattered the Muleshoe herd in the thick of the storm.

Criswell recalled, as he watched his herd shoved across the Red, how he and his boys had met up with Smith and his companions after the storm had petered out. They had a lurid tale to tell of how they had put Phillimore's cattle to running. They weren't sure as to whether they'd finished off that hellion Bryce, or whether they'd merely wounded him. Anyway, they'd set Phillimore's parcel of beef running fast through the storm and that was sufficient to delay the rival herd considerably.

There was something to be said for hiring gunslicks, reflected Criswell. Men like Sid Clifford might not exactly agree with him, but a cattleman had to fight hard for what he wanted. If it meant fighting in a not too clean fashion, then the fight must be carried on that way. There was no place for sentiment in this cattle-raising game in Jeff Criswell's view. He was in it to build a thriving outfit and catch quick financial returns and finer feelings could go to blazes!

Sid Clifford, on the other hand, rode with a brooding grudge. He remembered the way 'Joe Smith' and his gun-carrying friends had returned to the Spur Barb camp the night the Muleshoe herd had been stampeded in the storm. They were one man short in their number. He had been shot by the defenders of the Muleshoe herd and his body trampled in the first onslaught of stampeding beef, but he was a man who sold himself as a gunslinger, thus his death was taken as a matter of course in the Spur Barb ranks. Clifford remembered, as he rose, the way Smith and his companions boasted about the manner in which they had sent the rival herd thundering when they met up with the Spur Barb men after the event. It did not rest easy upon Clifford — or upon other out-and-out cowmen among the Spur Barb drovers — this knowledge that their employer was becoming more and more ruthless in the way he employed his gun-for-hire hellions.

It was true that Muleshoe had pulled off a smart-alecky trick at Mariposa Pass, but there had been no attempt at wanton murder from Jim Phillimore's men that night. With Criswell, it was different. He was out to kill, now, and no fine-sounding ethical considerations were going to stop him.

A streak of outright rebellion was working itself up to a critical point inside Sid Clifford, foreman of the Spur Barb outfit. Something of the same resentment was shared by other cow-hands who did not like the way the hired gunslingers were packing too much weight around the Spur Barb trail-crew.

It simmered deep inside them; but there was a time coming up when it would bust wide open!

Criswell had the crew push the herd some forty miles beyond the Red River, then slackened the pace. Smugly, he figured that he now had a far superior lead over the Muleshoe herd. After that little caper in the storm, he thought as he lighted his pipe close to the campfire at the chuck-wagon, Phillimore's herd probably split up into a couple of dozen minor herds and ran all night. No doubt, he mused, Jim Phillimore and his bunch were still on the Texas side of the Red River, vainly chasing hazing beef.

Criswell, with a deep satisfaction,

imagined that he'd steal that contract with the greatest of ease. He would have his herd into Dodge long before the Muleshoe bunch had even traversed the Indian Territory. Phillimore would miss the date and he, Jeff Criswell of Spur Barb, would be on hand to supply the contractor's need.

The future, he figured, was going to be tolerably rosy. No money for Phillimore out of this deal would mean that the Muleshoe rancher would be unable to retain lawyers to fight his land-claim case.

Jeff Criswell was mighty contented at that evening hour as he smoked his pipe at the chuck-wagon. It was almost a blessing that he didn't know exactly what was shaping in the immediate future, now that he had crossed into Indian Territory with his beef-on-the-hoof.

Far from being rosy, his future was going to be blood red!

11

When Pete Hiller said he had a smart little place all ready in which to tuck the stolen beef until their brands were blotted, he meant exactly what he said.

It was in the heart of Indian Territory, not too far removed from the major cattle-trails on which the rustler and his newly gathered bunch of cow-thieves hoped to prey during the new season. It was a hidden valley, a place which Hiller and the remainder of his old bunch had discovered in the days when they were on the owlhoot trail after a furious running fight with angry cowmen and the badge-toting upholders of United States' law. Discovery of the valley came as a heaven-sent reward to these men who deserved nothing from heaven.

No white man had ever entered it until they found the crack in the lines of high hills and craggy rock needles which was the gateway to the place. Wandering Indian bands might have known the place, but there was an abundance of game and fowl in the hidden valley, suggesting that no redmen had hunted within its walls for a long time.

It had everything a rustler crew could require and its best feature, so far as Hiller and his renegades were concerned, was its plentiful supply of good water. A broad ribbon of water flowed through the guarding walls of the hills and rock needles and there were slopes of good graze. It was exactly the place in which stolen cattle could be penned and kept, for weeks if need be, until their brands were blotted and changed so their owner would never recognise them.

Hiller and the remnants of his old bunch wintered in the valley. They cut the sparse timber which marched in straggling lines along the summits of the slopes and built a comfortable

180

cabin. Their sentries, posted high in the rock needles, had a wide view for miles, over which they could see the stirring of a trail herd or a posse when it was merely a speck of dust in the distance.

In the first days of spring, Hiller and his bunch emerged from their hibernation. In a quiet way, they began to marshal a new and stronger rustler crew, working from the almost forgotten town of Peak Crossing. This was another stage in the plans the rustler chieftain and his bunch had laid during their sojourn in their hidden winter quarters.

An earlier stage had been set in motion when Hiller's second-in-command, Rufe Hogan, had sallied forth from the isolated valley in the depth of winter to travel to Texas and take a look at the prospects offered by the ranchers down in the Lone Star State, who would be pushing their herds north for the railheads with the spring.

Pete Hiller had received a letter, sent by devious channels, in which Rufe had told him that he was now 'Joe Smith', that he had taken up with a Texas cowman who was hiring gunslingers, that he, Rufe Hogan, was in command of the gunslingers and that he was going to make the whole thing work out to Hiller's advantage by supplying him not only with the first beef catch of the new rustling season, but with a handful of newly recruited hardcases into the bargain.

Hence, when Jones and Britling rode into Peak Crossing with news from Rufe Hogan, Hiller and his small army of rustlers, intent upon action after a tough winter, loaded their sixguns and rode for the hidden valley.

Within its protecting walls, they began to make preparations for the two herds which Hogan had assured Hiller he would steer into the rustlers' laps. They built brush corrals, laid out branding-fires and kept a constant watch upon the unfolding distance from the secret places of the high rims.

There came an afternoon when Pete

Hiller, loafing against the cabin wall in pleasant sunshine, spotted one of his sentries waving a Winchester excitedly high in the rims, making himself visible only to the rustlers in the hidden valley. Hiller hastened up to the crest on which the man was posted. He saw, with glowing satisfaction, the sight for which he had long waited.

In the distance, small but very distinct, there was a rising column of dust. It was coming towards the hills in a lazily drifting pall.

'*Beef!*' rasped Hiller with an avaricious gleam in his eyes. '*That's beef, an' plenty of it!*'

'Must be a tolerable sized herd to raise that amount of dust,' murmured the sentry.

'It is,' confirmed Pete Hiller. 'That's one mighty big herd.'

The rustler chief fell silent, considering the far column of dust, eyes slitted against the glare of the high sun. He breathed a sigh of supreme satisfaction as a new item of interest caught his notice out beyond the swelling dust. 'Take a look out yonder, a bit towards the right of the dust,' he instructed the sentry.

The sentry gazed for a minute, slowly puckering his lips into a whistle as he watched.

'More dust — a long way off,' he commented. 'That's another herd, followin' the first pretty damn' fast.'

'Yeah,' grinned Hiller. 'Rufe wasn't jokin' when he said he'd have two herds for us to tuck away. They're both comin' fast. Looks like we're goin' back into business in a big way!'

* * *

Jeff Criswell would never have rested his herd for an instant once he had forded the Red if he knew how hard his rival from the Llano Diablo country was shoving his herd on the Spur Barb back-trail. Jim Phillimore, helped by a crew of mightily determined wranglers, was shoving the beef in a way in which

184

he had never driven cattle before.

Powered by its cold determination to even up with Spur Barb, the Muleshoe crew was tearing up the dust of Indian Territory in a near superhuman effort to be at the railhead in Dodge City before Criswell and his dirty-dealing outfit.

Across the Red, they advanced by pushing the beef half the night, giving the cattle only the minimum amount of rest and grazing. Criswell, on the other hand, bedded the Spur Barb herd for a full night. His men had ridden hard and punched cows hard. There was a distinctly ugly mood in them, Criswell noted, particularly in Sid Clifford, his foreman. Maybe, since they had made good time, catching up on the mileage lost when Muleshoe pulled its trick at Mariposa Pass, he had better give them a reasonable rest. He'd seen weary men with frayed tempers on the trail before; they became even more fractious than the cattle and fist-fights, sometimes even gunplay, flared easily. On this drive, he had enough to cope with without that kind of trail-camp trouble.

So, he rested his herd and his men for a full night, little realizing that Muleshoe had made a good recovery from the depredations of the night of the storm and was not so far behind as he imagined.

His outfit made an almost sluggish start the following morning. Was it his imagination or were Joe Smith and the rest of the hired gunnies deliberately trying to delay the start of the herd?

Smith claimed his wallet was missing just after breakfast and there was a strained moment of tension when the regular Spur Barb hands wanted to know if Smith was trying to say there was a thief among their number. Criswell only just stopped a fist-fight between one of the hired gunmen and old Sid Clifford who had been powerful cantankerous these last couple of days and was ready to defend the good name of the Spur Barb men.

Then, the better part of an hour was

lost as men beat around the grass in the place where Smith spread his bed-roll the night before. When all this effort to find the wallet proved fruitless, Smith suddenly showed up and said he'd found the wallet in his saddle-bag, having put it there the previous day and forgetting he had done so.

The upshot of the whole thing was that the Spur Barb herd began its trek late that morning, but it pushed steadily along and, by the afternoon, a line of hills and rugged rock needles was rearing to the north of the travelling beef.

Something else was rising behind the Spur Barb herd: a thin pall of dust, marking the steady approach of a second bunch of cattle out of Texas. Criswell and his crew were unaware of it for a long time, but there were men watching from the high needles up ahead who viewed this column of hoof-risen dust with the greatest of interest, just as they viewed that which the Spur Barb herd sent into the heat-charged air.

The Spur Barb wranglers whooped the cattle along steadily through the sultry afternoon. In the late afternoon, there was a yell from up front of the herd as somebody called for Jeff Criswell.

Criswell, who was with the drag riders well down the stream of horn-tipped heads, took his cow pony up ahead. He found Sid Clifford and a knot of Spur Barb men showing great interest in a string of quickly advancing dots placed between the herd and the far line of ragged country.

Those dots were horsemen, a whole line of horsemen coming at the herd on a wide front, almost with the speed of a troop of attacking cavalry.

Criswell didn't like the look of them. They were small at this distance, but they were certainly whites and not trouble-making Indians.

The owner of Spur Barb was so intent on the approaching line of riders that he failed to notice a significant point: Smith and his gunslingers had all been riding close to the head of the herd. They had been there for most of the afternoon, as if watching for something. Now, as the string of riders grew in the middle distance, racing across the tawny land towards the trail-herd, Smith and two more of his men remained up at the head, but the remainder dropped back to take up unobtrusive positions near the scattered clumps of Spur Barb cowboys.

'What's this mean?' asked Criswell, screwing his wrinkle-fringed eyes and studying the rapidly growing riders.

'Maybe a posse after someone,' murmured Clifford. 'Maybe they want to ask us if we've seen the feller they're lookin' for.'

'If that's a posse, then the feller they're lookin' for must've murdered the President,' rumbled one of the cowhands. 'Never saw a posse that big in my life. It's damn near a small army!'

The approaching riders grew. There was a strong note of danger in the way they presented a fanned-out front and the sun put a bright glitter on repeaters and sixguns flourishing in their hands.

A dry chuckle came from behind the backs of Criswell. Clifford and the rest of the Spur Barb men up at the head of the herd and the double rasp of metal leaving leather followed it.

Criswell, Clifford and their Spur Barb companions turned their heads to see that the man they knew as Joe Smith and a couple of the hired gunslingers had pranced their horses into a strategic position at their backs — and these men held the mouths of their drawn pistols levelled at them. Criswell made a hasty move for the Colt at his belt, but 'Smith' wagged the revolver in his hand in a disapproving fashion.

'Don't you try nothin' of that sort, old man,' he warned the rancher. 'This shootin' iron is liable to go off an' I don't want to set them cows of yours a-runnin' until we're ready to run 'em. That'll be when the fellers you see ridin' this way have reached us.'

Jeff Criswell's Adam's apple bobbed up and down in his scrawny neck and Sid Clifford sat his horse with his hands well away from his gun and his face a mask of outright hatred for 'Smith' and his companions. His mistrust of the hired gunslingers had been proved well-founded. He had long ago observed that 'Joe Smith' seemed to be taking over the running of the Spur Barb trail-herd. Now, the gunslinger had certainly accomplished a take-over. His companions of the gun-for-sale persuasion were dotted all along the trail, covering groups of Spur Barb wranglers, just as Criswell and the foreman were being covered.

The cattle, in their unknowing, bovine way, were streaming past, horn-to-horn as the drama was acted out with the Spur Barb men held immobile and the madly-riding crew of gunmen approaching across the vast country.

Criswell overcame his moment of blank stupidity.

'What're you tryin' to do, Smith?' he rasped.

'Ain't tryin' to do anythin',' the gunslinger informed him. 'We've done it — we've taken over your herd an' the fellers you see headin' this way are comin' to clinch the deal in a business-like fashion. That's Pete Hiller an' his boys!'

'Hiller!' exclaimed Jeff Criswell. 'So you been workin' with Hiller all along — fixin' to make this grab at my beef!'

Rufe Hogan allowed a hard grin to take control of his doughy face. It was a grin without humour.

'You've cottoned on to the idea, Mr Criswell. I was never really much interested in your fool feud with Phillimore. I was interested in steerin' this parcel of beef into this particular part of the Indian Territory an' helpin' to do the same thing for the Muleshoe herd. If it's any consolation to you, Phillimore's cattle is goin' to be rustled just like yours when it gets here. My name, by the way, is Rufe Hogan. Not that you'll ever be able to tell your friends about meetin' the great Pete

Hiller an' his sidekick, Hogan, because you an' all your boys will be plumb dead.'

The man immediately behind Hogan, sitting in his saddle with a six-shooter pointed squarely at Criswell and Clifford, smirked and, at that moment, the pent-up hatred which had grown in Sid Clifford through these past few hours boiled over.

He saw the iniquity of the whole thing. He saw how Spur Barb had taken these vipers into its bunkhouse to work their poison in a ranch which had once been decent, enjoying a good reputation until Criswell became a greedy old man and stooped to the depths of barbed wire and hired gunsharps. And this was the end of it all: a smart-alecky trick in which the hired gunmen held the trail-drovers at pistol point while the notorious Pete Hiller and a small army of rustlers came to steal the herd.

Red rage flared in Clifford. He could hear the thundering of the approaching rustlers' horses, a sound which seemed to portend the approach of death. There was something in the hard, merciless smirk of the man behind Hogan which sparked the foreman into wild action.

Swearing on a near-hysterical note, he clawed for the gun holstered at his waist.

Criswell saw him move and tried to stop him with a squeaky cry.

Hogan turned his six-gun directly at Clifford, his pasty face set in bleak lines, like a mask of carved granite. He said coldly:

'You just got yourself killed, you old — ' The last of the sentence was buried in the blasting cough of the Colt.

Sid Clifford, square-shooting cow-puncher, but no gunsharp, had just cleared leather with his pistol when Hogan's bullet tore through his heart. He stiffened in the saddle with a last gusty sigh, dropped the gun from dead fingers and flopped over the saddle-horn like a doll stuffed with sawdust, held on the horse's back by boots hooked in the worn, Texas-style wooden stirrups.

Criswell jerked up straight as a ramrod in his saddle, staring at the dead Clifford with unbelieving eyes. Smoke issued from Hogan's Colt in a thin string. There was a nervous stirring among the cattle after the slam of the gun and, for a moment, it looked as though they might start running.

But there was suddenly a bunch of riders, flanking the herd, riding them into orderly submission at the fringe of the sea of horn-barbed heads, where they tended to panic and break away. These were Hiller's riders, his small army of cattle-thieves, who had now reached the Spur Barb herd.

In the dusty confusion, loud with the grunts and bawls of startled animals, Jeff Criswell was shouting abuse at Rufe Hogan who merely retained his smirking smile. Criswell had valued Sid Clifford and, though the rancher and foreman had lately had a grinding discontent between them, the part of

Criswell that was still all-out cowman knew that Clifford had been right. Now, Clifford was dead at the hands of these scheming hellions and Criswell's herd was about to be stolen in broad daylight by the biggest rustler bunch ever to operate along the cattle-trails.

A mounted man came thrusting his animal through the confused scattering of cattle, a man built like a gorilla with elegant, dandified touches to his gear — Pete Hiller, the rustler boss. Hiller walked his horse towards the point where Criswell and the knot of Spur Barb men who had been riding at the head of the herd were immobile under the guns of Rufe Hogan and his companions. He was glowering at Hogan and there seemed to be little in the way of a friendly welcome for the Hiller bunch's second-in-command.

'What the hell d'you think you're doin', shootin' off a gun that way?' bawled Hiller.

Hogan indicated the dead Clifford slumped in his saddle.

'That old fool tried to draw his iron on me,' he said coldly.

Hiller snorted. 'D'you want to tell the whole damned Territory what's goin' on up this way?' he demanded. 'That bunch back yonder must've heard you shoot — d' you want to put them on their guard?' As he spoke, Hiller jerked his thumb back and indicated something which Hogan and his cronies and the Spur Barb men, too, were now seeing for the first time: a growing column of hoof-risen dust, removed from the Spur Barb herd by only a few miles.

'Muleshoe!' Rufe Hogan almost gurgled. 'I didn't figure they could be this near!'

'Well, they are this near, an' I aim to grab every last head of beef they're pushin', provided you don't go warnin' 'em with your blasted pistol shots that we're making our play up here,' Hiller rasped.

'Sorry, Pete,' rumbled the chastened Hogan. 'I figured I'd best shoot first an' stop that crazy old galoot — he was foreman of this crew an' he would have ventilated me if he got that shootin'-iron clear fast enough.' Hogan shrugged his shoulders and his hard grin spread over the doughy features. 'Still, what's one old galoot dead at this stage? We're goin' to finish all of 'em off, ain't we? You can't go allowin' 'em to run around loose after we've taken the beef, so they can bring the law out this way, can you?'

'An' I ain't goin' to scatter 'em all over the Territory so the law can come snoopin' around when someone comes ridin' along, has his attention caught by a parcel of buzzards an' discovers a bundle of corpses,' Hiller responded tartly. 'I'll finish this crew off in my own way, an' in the valley where nobody is goin' to find the evidence. None of that is to the point, anyway. I don't like you shootin' an' warnin' that Muleshoe crew. I want them to fall for our move as easy as this crew did.'

The captured Spur Barb rancher and his men glowered at the heavily built man in elegant range-garb, who proposed to finish them off 'in his own way'. Exactly what that phrase meant, they had no way of knowing, but stories about the cold-blooded cruelty of Pete Hiller and his rustler outfit had been retailed far and wide over the cattle country. Whatever the rustler chieftain had in store for them would be far from pleasant, they felt.

The prospect prompted a question from Jeff Criswell. The old rancher was not cowed by the rustler bunch; he sat his saddle with a certain dignity to his bony frame and there was all the belligerent spirit of a Texan cut from the old rock in his face as he asked:

'What're you aimin' to do with my men an' me?'

'You'll find out soon enough!' snarled Hiller. 'Meantime, hand over your shootin'-irons to my men an' don't try any monkey tricks or you'll wind up just as dead as your foreman there. Then bunch yourselves together, my men are goin' to ride you an' your cows into a quiet restin' place.' Hiller turned his attention to a segment of his small army of cow-thieves. 'All right, you *hombres*, get this cattle headed for the valley. Take them an' these fellers into the valley fast. We want to get 'em out of sight before the Muleshoe crew shows up — an' they'll be here sooner than we realize,' he ordered.

'I don't know what the hell you're up to, by grab, but you won't get away with it this easy!' bawled Jeff Criswell in furious anger as a rustler took his Colt from its holster.

'Save your breath,' said Hiller harshly. 'We have no time to listen to your empty bluster. We have another herd to snatch this afternoon an' I don't figure it will be steered into our pockets the way yours was.'

Swearing with bitter frustration, the Spur Barb men rode into a bunch under the ready guns of Pete Hiller's men. Hiller made the disarmed cow wranglers take the horse bearing the corpse of Sid Clifford with them. He sent the captives ahead of the herd under a heavy guard, placed riders along the herd and turned prisoners and stolen cattle for the line of hills and rock needles.

'Make it snappy!' he thundered as the mass of beef began to head off in the new direction. 'That Muleshoe dust is gettin' nearer an' I want this outfit plumb out of sight before they see what we're up to!'

The rustlers whooped the herd into travelling fast.

Pete Hiller had opened his new season of rustling and today was going to be a fruitful one for him.

So he thought.

12

The hand of destiny touched the Muleshoe herd that sun-pounded afternoon as it shifted, protesting with loud lowing sounds from tipped-back horn-barbed heads with the wranglers riding hard. This herd was moving like no beef-on-the-hoof had moved across the vast sprawl of Indian Territory before. It was raising choking dust and there wasn't a 'puncher in the crew who wouldn't have given a whole month's wages for a beer and a quiet smoke under a good shade tree.

But they had a mission to accomplish. They were making good time and the Spur Barb herd, for all its advantage, taken when the Muleshoe beef was stampeded that night in the lashing storm, could not be far ahead. There was a vigorous spirit to the manner in which the Muleshoe drovers were shoving the cattle; it was a spirit shared by old Jim Phillimore in no small degree. Time was when men said Jim was getting old and was not the old Jim Phillimore of years before. But these days in the saddle and this furious fight to reach Dodge before his neighbour from the Llano Diablo ranges had brought out much of the old drover of the early trail days in Phillimore.

Men who had ridden with him for years noted with satisfaction that the tough old Texan's face seemed to have lost its haggard appearance as it was turned against the sun, beard jutting and eyes scrunched against the fierce light, when Phillimore bellowed orders to this company of men who forced the cattle along at a pace which raised the dust of Indian Territory higher than any beef ever raised it before.

To Dan Bryce, riding with a wounded arm and thinking dark thoughts of vengeance, Phillimore looked once more like that same Jim Phillimore who had come storming into that bloodthirsty crew of trailmen back in Fannin City with a tough-fisted company of wranglers at his back. A damned good galoot, was old Jim, thought Bryce, and his whole outfit was a mighty good one. It would be a pity if a snake like Jeff Criswell scored over him and stole that beef contract at the Dodge City railhead.

A pity, too, that this drive had its share of violence and brutality: the bad start with the night-herders murdered on the eve of the departure and the stampede in which Mex Salinas had been killed.

Dan Bryce's grudge against Spur Barb for the killing of Salinas ground at him in time to the steady throbbing of the wound in his arm. He'd get even for that, just as soon as he met up with the Spur Barb crew, he promised himself for the thousandth time. He wanted Rufe Hogan, who was known at Spur Barb as 'Joe Smith', for the killing of Salinas. When he caught sight of the Spur Barb herd, he would ride out alone and fix Hogan the way he needed fixing — at the end of a sixgun and in front of the man who had hired him to do dirty work for trigger money.

The hand of destiny was on the Muleshoe trail crew that afternoon when young Ben Grimes, once a Spur Barb rider, caught sight of a banner of dust spiralling thinly in a grey mass far ahead of the rapidly travelling Muleshoe beef.

At first, the young wrangler thought it was smoke and wondered if the red men were getting up to their well known tricks: then, he realized that it was the dust of the Spur Barb herd.

He was riding at the head of the Muleshoe herd and he brought his mount to a splay-footed halt while he shielded his eyes with his hand and took a longer look at the far drift of risen dust.

'It's their herd, all right,' he confirmed to himself, then he waved to Dan Bryce, riding close behind.

'Spur Barb up ahead!' he yelled.

'We're makin' better time than we know!'

Bryce came cantering up, following Grimes' pointing finger and noting the rising dust as he rode. He felt a lift of spirits. So, Spur Barb was just a few miles away — well, he'd go right ahead and even up for Mex Salinas in his own devil-be-damned way!

He took his sixgun from its leather and checked its chambers.

The news that the rival herd was in sight rippled down the line of Muleshoe wranglers. Jim Phillimore came riding up from the drag lines, squinting excitedly at the interesting smudge rising high against the sun-burnished blue of the sky. He saw Bryce shoving his well-maintained gun back into its holster, read a meaning into the coldly determined expression of the face of the man in black.

'What're you aimin' to do?' he wanted to know.

'Aimin' to do a little chore,' said Bryce. 'Aimin' to go an' look in on the

Spur Barb rannihans an' even up for Mex Salinas. There's a galoot ridin' with Criswell who was just born to be shot an' I aim to ride in an' shoot him. The feller who set our beef to stampedin' in the storm an' the feller who caused Mex Salinas to be trampled.'

'Smith?' asked Charlie Manders who had paced his bronc up behind Phillimore's.

'It's high time someone ventilated him an' I figure I'll go an' do it,' said Dan quietly.

'Wait a minute,' protested Jim Phillimore. 'You got a slug in your arm. If there's any shootin' to be done, we'll come up an' help you.'

'There's nothin' wrong with my arm an' I do the shootin' alone,' Bryce stated with an edge of coldness to his voice. 'Your job is to get this parcel of beef to Dodge in time to meet a date. Go right ahead an' do it. My job is to shoot, remember. You hired my gun, Jim, and we've fooled around on the edge of this thing long enough. Now it's

207

time for shootin'. I saw the face of the guy who led that bunch on the night of the storm. He fired the shot that set the critters runnin', now I'm goin' up the trail to shoot him.'

The man from New Mexico said it in a way which hinted he had heard enough contradictions.

'I don't want to see you ride into Spur Barb's clutches an' get yourself killed, you damn' fool,' persisted Jim Phillimore.

'I'll take my chances,' said Bryce, touching his knees to the ribs of his bronc.

He took the tough little animal away from the herd at a brisk rate, the protests of Phillimore and his men falling on his deaf ears. Jim Phillimore snorted indignantly: 'He's plumb stupid. That young feller survived near murder back in Fannin City when he was just a kid, but, by the horny toad, I don't think he'll survive what he's shovin' his neck into with a crazy move like he's makin' now.'

'He learned a few tricks in his time, Jim,' said Charlie Manders gravely. 'I reckon he knows what he's doin'.'

Sitting their saddles in silence, the Muleshoe men watched Bryce's riding figure dwindle against the vast land as he headed for the smear of dust floating against the bright sky.

For all his hasty riding, Dan Bryce travelled with eyes and ears alert. Every step of the bronc brought him nearer to hostile men and there might be a few Spur Barb stragglers, idling in the rear of the drive, who could spot him. He wanted to do this thing without giving Criswell's crew too much premature warning. He was determined to smoke it out with Rufe Hogan, man-to-man, right in the camp of the rancher who had hired the dough-faced gunslinger.

The grinding nag of the bandaged slug-nick in his arm kept pace with the pounding of blood at his temples. All the piled up fury that had mounted in him since he saw the pulped remains of

209

Mex Salinas lifted out of the hoof-mauled mud in the slashing storm was prodding at him. It was the vengeful Dan Bryce of the Hix Creek ruckus; the rip-roaring Dan Bryce who, sprawled on the boardwalk of a New Mexico township, had smoked it out with Dutch Kloot's crew, who now rode towards the Spur Barb herd with a ready gun to back his blazing temper.

The vast land, with its ridges and folds, had put the Muleshoe trail outfit out of sight at his back and the rising dust which marked the rival herd was nearer when he heard a shot. It was the sudden blast of a sixgun slamming a flat clap through the heat-charged air. It came from some point quite near just as the lone rider had dropped down into a hollow of land. He came up the rise of the far side of the hollow, then checked his bronc's progress so that it did not reach the rim of the upward slope and man and horse were not skylined.

Bryce's swift action in halting the

horse was prompted by the loud, seemingly close chorus of many grunting animals. The Spur Barb herd was much nearer than he had imagined but he had been following it only by the betraying ribbon of dust, the folding and up-ended land of this region, close to a line of hills and rock needles, having hitherto hidden the Spur Barb trail outfit from view. But, in cresting the rise, Bryce had been given his first glimpse of Criswell's bunch, down on the trail beyond the rise, the cows more or less halted.

It was from that direction that the solitary shot had echoed and the brief glimpse of the Spur Barb bunch which Dan had been afforded before he yanked his animal back down the slope, showed him that something was wrong. Angry voices floated up to him above the sound of the restless herd and he saw a man he thought was Jeff Criswell sitting on horseback arguing with another mounted man who held him at pistol point.

Moreover, there was a small army of

mounted men, fanning out on a wide front, riding hell-for-leather towards the Spur Barb herd from the direction of the line of hills.

Bryce dropped the rein of his bronc over its head to hang against its forelegs and prevent it from straying, left it in the hollow while he climbed up the rise again, dropping to a crouch as he neared the top, then flattening down on his stomach as he reached the summit.

Looking down through clumps of high grown wild grass and rock clutters, he could just see the sluggishly moving herd below.

Criswell and a company of cowhands were all confronted by men who levelled sixguns at them; Bryce felt that the one who sat his horse opposite Jeff Criswell and held the mouth of his gun directed at the rancher was Rufe Hogan, but he couldn't be sure at this distance. Voices were rising in a thin hubbub in which it was impossible to distinguish the words — and the small army of tough looking riders, who,

Bryce could now see, flourished six-guns and rifles as they headed for the Spur Barb herd, were moving fast and with the precision of horse-soldiers.

Coldly, Bryce recalled that Rufe Hogan had been known as the right hand man of the arch-rustler Pete Hiller. This drama smacked suspiciously of a cattle snatch, he thought, as he watched the way the riders from the hills fanned out and came down upon the herd.

There was a scattering of rocks and closely-grown thorn clumps some distance down the slope. Bryce figured that, if he could 'Injun' his way down the slope to that sparse cover, he would be able to overhear what was going on down at the herd. Earlier, he had nurtured ideas of riding right up to the Spur Barb crew and having it out with Hogan face to face, but this new development cooled his hot temper to the extent that he realized that even he, Dan Bryce of the supposed charmed life, could not go prodding into the mob of hard-cases down yonder and live to tell the tale.

He slithered on his stomach through the long grass, going carefully but swiftly. He reached the clump of rock and thorn and squatted there, a matter of yards away from the Spur Barb drovers and the men who had so obviously jumped them and their beef.

The riders who had come from the direction of the hills at such a rapid lick had now reached the herd, they were pushing some rebellious cows back into line and riding back and to, soothing cattle which showed signs of the jitters, probably because of the shot which had been loosed off so close to them.

Squinting through the thorn, Dan realized that the man mounted next to Jeff Criswell was slumped slackly over his saddle horn in the way of a dead man on horseback. He remembered the solitary shot which had echoed over the rugged land and he pursed his lips. He could see, too, that the man who held old Criswell under his gun was Rufe

Hogan, otherwise Joe Smith. He saw a heavily built man with touches of elegant trappings here and there on his range garb, riding through the cattle and approaching Hogan. The man's face was one which he had seen time and time again on the reward posters put out by the various cattlemen's protection societies. It was the face of Pete Hiller.

Hiller was shouting angrily at Hogan and Bryce heard the words:

'*What the hell d'you think you're doin', shootin' off a gun that way?*'

He heard Hogan's response, spoken as he waved his gun towards the dead man on horseback: '*That old fool tried to draw his iron on me.*'

Pete Hiller raised his arm and pointed beyond the very slope on which Bryce crouched behind the rock and thorn. The rustler chief bellowed: '*Do you want to tell the whole damned Territory what's goin' on up this way? That bunch back yonder must've heard you shoot — d'you want to put them on their guard?'*

The concealed man saw Hogan look back at the direction indicated by the rustler leader and he knew that he was looking at the rise of dust from the approaching Muleshoe herd before he heard Hogan's ejaculation: *'Muleshoe! I didn't figure they could be this near!'*

Bryce heard Hiller's voice rasp out a sentence of highly interesting content: *'Well, they are this near, an' I aim to grab every last head of beef they're pushin', provided you don't go warnin' 'em with your blasted pistol shots that we're makin' our play up here.'*

There was a muttered interlude between Hiller and Hogan during which Bryce saw the rustler gang's second-in-command indicate the dead man slumped grotesquely in his saddle and heard him remark: *' . . . he was foreman of this crew an' he would have ventilated me if he got that shootin'-iron clear fast enough.'* Hogan shrugged his shoulders and added: *'Still, what's one old galoot dead at this stage? We're goin' to finish all of 'em off ain't we?'*

Dan listened intently to the reply rasped by Pete Hiller and there was one observation which he placed away securely in his memory. Hiller said: *'I'll finish this crew off in my own way, an' in the valley where nobody is goin' to find the evidence . . .'*

Bryce hugged the ground in the lee of the rock and thorn cover. He watched the rustlers rounding up Spur Barb riders and force them to the head of the herd as prisoners. He noticed that among the men who held the Criswell wranglers under armed guard were those who had been hired by the owner of Spur Barb to fight for trigger-wages in the feud against Muleshoe. The situation was as plain as day to him. He saw that Rufe Hogan, and the hired gunsharps Jeff Criswell had taken on the ranch's payroll, were playing a double game under Hogan's guidance. They were in cahoots with Hiller and they had steered the Spur Barb beef right into Hiller's clutches.

More, they intended to go right out after the approaching Muleshoe herd when they had tucked this one safely away in a location to which Pete Hiller had referred as 'the valley'.

He remembered the way he had seen the small army of Hiller's rustlers come splitting the wind from the direction of the line of hills and needles in the distance and, now, the prisoners and their cattle were being marshalled in that direction. The answer came to Dan without the exercise of a great deal of mental effort. Hidden valleys and secluded coulees were the delight of all rustlers who, especially in country which would soon be crowded with cows and cowmen as the spring herding season opened fully, needed a place to blot the brands of rustled stock. Indian Territory abounded with such places and Pete Hiller, back in business once more, must have discovered such a place.

It was somewhere in that distant line of rearing formations.

Hiller was taking the Spur Barb herd and the Spur Barb wranglers there. He would make money out of the herd when he shifted it into some distant market with altered brands, but he would kill Jeff Criswell and his riders.

Dan Bryce knew that when Hiller spoke of killing the men where there would be no evidence of the crime, he meant every word of it. Pete Hiller had a killer streak a mile wide running through him and he was already wanted for murder committed in the earlier stages of his career as a cattle thief. If the law ever caught up with Hiller, he would stretch rope, anyway, so he entertained no scruples about taking human life.

And there was a further point about this affair which held Dan Bryce's attention. Among the men who rode with Hiller, he had spotted a familiar face and the thought came to him that part of his past had emerged in this business in which he had sold his gun for the protection of Jim Phillimore's

Muleshoe outfit.

The face was that of Kid Billings, last of the Dutch Kloot outlaw bunch. Kid was a no-account rannihan, but Bryce knew he had been mixed up in the vicious killings perpetrated by Kloot's gunthrowing scum. It seemed that part of his lawman's work undertaken in Cholla remained undone so long as Kid Billings remained alive and he knew that Billings was vicious enough to want to put him out of the way — provided he could do it with the maximum amount of safety for Kid Billings. Bryce felt an itch to give Billings what was coming to him both for the brutal killings in Arizona in which he'd been involved and for the cowardly way he'd left Haffner to meet death alone in the dusty street of Cholla.

But that was a minor consideration. From his perch behind the rocks and thorn bushes, he watched the rustlers make away with their prisoners and stolen stock. He noticed a streak of old

Texan stubbornness in the way Jeff Criswell accepted defeat. He even felt sorry for the owner of Spur Barb and his riders. He remembered the way the obviously square-shooting cowmen had stood aloof from the gun-for-hire ruffians at the bar that night in the Double Ace back in the Llano Diablo country.

Criswell might have played a far from clean game in his feud with big Jim Phillimore, but the cantankerous old rancher had certainly nursed a viper to his bosom when he took Hogan and the rest of the gunslingers on to his payroll.

He knew that he could not leave these men to be slaughtered by the bloodthirsty army of gun-heavy drifters which Pete Hiller had gathered about him to add further gory pages to his career; he knew that Hiller's crew would soon be back over this country to make a grab at the unsuspecting Muleshoe herd.

Dan watched the dust haze in the backtrail of the dwindling Spur Barb herd now being driven towards the hills by the rustlers. He waited until the departing herd was far enough away to ensure that distance and the fog of dust hid his movements. Then, he sprang up from his hiding place, hared up the harsh grass of the slope, rimmed it, ran down the other side and forked his bronc waiting in the hollow.

Riding as though every kill-crazy Indian in creation was on his tail, he travelled for the banner of dust which indicated the approaching Muleshoe herd.

13

Back at the Muleshoe herd, they took the news gravely, the owner of the outfit and his wranglers sitting their mounts around the newly returned Dan Bryce.

Big Jim Phillimore tugged at his beard, repeating the information which Bryce had brought: 'Taken Criswell and his crew an 'aim to kill 'em, eh? Shot poor old Sid Clifford, did they? Got a small army of hellions all set to jump my herd, huh?'

Charlie Manders, foreman of Muleshoe, shifted uneasily in his battered El Paso saddle.

'It's a hell of a thing — shootin' old Sid,' he commented. 'He was all right. I knew him for years.' He thumped his Colt loose in its holster with an unconscious action as he spoke.

'Sure, Sid was the best feller on the

Spur Barb spread,' murmured young Ben Grimes.

A fighting mood was spreading rapidly through the Muleshoe ranks. If Pete Hiller thought he was going to take this bunch of beef easily, said the wranglers to themselves, he had better think again. Then there was the matter of the fate of the Spur Barb men.

Old rock Texas toughness was showing in the face of Jim Phillimore. He sat his saddle as solid as a mountain and thrust his spiky beard defiantly forward. Bryce thought that, more than ever, he looked like the fighting Jim Phillimore of old who had come thundering into a saloon brawl back in Fannin City years before.

'I got no love for Jeff Criswell,' he said huskily. 'I don't know if he was behind the shootin' up of my night-herders or if it was that feller who called himself Smith an' I don't know if he condoned the stampedin' of our herd durin' that storm. I don't like his business methods an' I don't like his wire fences, but, damn it, him an' me have been neighbours for years, even if we've spent a lot of time fightin'. I can't see him an' his boys butchered by Hiller's murderin' crew without a hope of defendin' themselves. We've got to do somethin' about it!'

'We'll do somethin', all right,' nodded Dan Bryce. 'An' we've got to do somethin' about Hiller's forthcomin' attempt to grab our beef. He an' his hellions will be here before we know it an' we'll have to act fast.'

There was a spontaneous whisking of Winchesters from saddle-scabbards and lifting of Colts from holsters among the Muleshoe hands. They checked magazines and slipped cartridges from their belt loops into sixgun chambers.

'Got any ideas, Dan?' asked Phillimore.

'Got one which might pay off if we move quick an' get the jump on Hiller,' Bryce answered. 'It'll mean movin' this herd a bit further up towards those humps in the land an' not goin' over 'em. We'll have to hole the cattle up on this side of the humps, ready for when Hiller an' his men come out of their hills an' cross the humps. If we get the beef moved fast an' lay 'em out right, we'll give Pete Hiller an' his rannihans the shock of their sweet lives!'

He outlined a quick plan of action to Phillimore and the Muleshoe men and another five minutes saw them hollering at the beef-on-the-hoof once more, pushing the stock along and raising plenty of dust.

* * *

Pete Hiller grinned with satisfaction as he brought the spearhead of his madly-riding rustler crew towards the folds of land which furrowed this section of the country into a series of humps. Beyond the first of those humps, the banner of dust which marked the oncoming Muleshoe herd was a dark splotch against the sun-brightened sky. Phillimore's herd was very near, thought Hiller, and the bearded old rancher from the Llano Diablo country could have no idea that the biggest army of cow-thieves this territory had ever known was on its way to make the second large scale cattle robbery of that day.

The Spur Barb stock, and its drovers, were now secure in the hidden valley. Hiller aimed to deal with Criswell and his men in his own decisive way when he got back with this new bunch of stolen beef. Then he'd get round to blotting the brands of both Spur Barb and Muleshoe cattle, the whole of the four-legged longhorn booty making a spectacular haul even for the audacious Hiller who had no lack of previous spectacular exploits to his credit.

For the time being, Jeff Criswell and his drovers were under a guard of rustlers in the valley.

Hiller knew that Phillimore and his men would make a fight when the rustlers attempted to jump the herd. Phillimore, though he might be growing old, was the type of Texan who was likely to lose his fighting spirit only when he was dead; furthermore, there was no 'inside' co-operation in Muleshoe herd such as had been furnished by Rufe Hogan and the rest of the gunsharps who rode with Criswell. Nobody was going to steer the Muleshoe cattle right into Pete Hiller's greedy hands the way the Spur Barb beef had been. Then, there was the matter of that *hombre* Dan Bryce. The stories had it that Bryce had cleaned up the Hix Creek rustler bunch almost single-handed, that he was death to rustlers and hell on wheels with a gun.

Hiller was scornful of the stories about all 'reputation' gunmen with solid reason for being so. It was a matter of simple truth that a man who had enjoyed some minor success with his sixgun, perhaps through nothing but luck, acquired an aura of greatness and highly embroidered tales went the rounds. Hiller was a realist, and he felt that Bryce might be just another cardboard hero with more luck than gun-savvy. Rufe Hogan had told the rustler boss that he had set out one dark night to finish off the hero of Hix Creek and Hogan had been honest enough to admit that, while he was sure he had hit Bryce with his Winchester slug, he did not know whether he had killed him.

Anyway, Pete Hiller told himself, they would soon know whether Bryce was still alive. And they would soon know just how much those yarns about him were worth.

For the Hiller bunch, having secured the Spur Barb beef and its wranglers in the valley, were streaming out of the line of hills at a hell-for-leather lick, spreading out into a wide front as they neared the humps of earth beyond which soared the tell-tale smudge of hoof-risen dust.

Pete Hiller had been at the rustling game long enough to have developed into a reasonably good general. He had devised a method of swooping directly down upon a herd on a wide front so that his riders could swiftly encircle the beef and its attendant wranglers.

This was the move he was now going to employ as his crew thundered over the sun-punished and parched land of Indian Territory, making for that column of dust just beyond the first of the humps in the terrain.

They reached the hump and went splitting the wind, riding furiously up the slanting land, flourishing sixguns and carbines. They crested the rise with Hiller riding a little to the fore like a cavalry commander leading his men full at the enemy.

On the crest of the hump, just as his horse was dropping down the far side of the fold in the land, Hiller and his hellions received what Dan Bryce had forecast as the 'shock of their sweet lives'.

For, in the midst of their headlong horseback plunge, they saw that they were confronted by a superior and formidable force. Something much more fearsome than mere armed men waited just over the hump, only a matter of a few yards from them. Hiller had known from the rising dust that the Muleshoe trail herd was near. But he had not imagined it to be this near.

And never in his wildest dreams had he ever expected to encounter a herd laid out as this one was.

For it was not strung along the trail in the usual fashion, with riders deployed at the head of the drive and at strategic points along it. It was lined up on a front broader than that of Hiller's attacking party. A great, deep wall of hundreds of Texas long-horns confronted the rustlers as they came at breakneck speed over the rise; a wall of stolidly moving cattle which made Hiller's attacking force appear puny.

Phillimore and his drovers were riding at the back of the ranks of horn-tipped heads with revolvers and carbines ready, shoving the cattle along with harsh whoops. Belatedly, Pete Hiller saw the significance of the

Muleshoe men's position and realized exactly what kind of move they were about to make. He yanked leather furiously and attempted to haul his unnerved horse about, bawling for his plunging riders to beat a retreat.

His panicky orders were lost in a storm of wild Texan yells and the crackling blasts of carbines and side-arms as Phillimore's crew loosed a tumultuous racket at the back of the onward plodding herd. The fury of sound had the only effect that such a concerted din could have on a tight-packed mass of cattle. Panic ripped along the horn barbed spearhead of beasts lumbering up the slope to meet the rustlers who were now tangled in a desperate effort to pull their mounts around and haze back the way they had come.

The quivering panic of the hundreds of head of cattle whispered through their ranks for a brief instant of tension fraught time.

Then it broke in a thundering

onslaught of drumming hoofs.

Carbines and sixguns blasted and roared again at the rear of the running cattle and, for the rustlers, making their mad attempt to ride back over the hill, the whole world seemed to be torn apart by the force of the stampede. The Muleshoe cattle were coming at them on a vast front, running faster than they ran the night Rufe Hogan and his gunsharps stampeded them in the teeth of the storm; running like a herd out of hell, tearing at the dry ground with a tremendous tempest of mauling hoofs.

The danger threatened the Hiller bunch only. They faced the great, massed power of a crazily running herd of panicking beef while the men of the Muleshoe outfit came behind it, goading the stampede onwards. Grinning whitely in the fog of dust at the back of the wall of speeding cattle, they rode madly, yelling and shooting.

Hiller was lost in a floundering sea of frightened horses. His men were trying to control their scared mounts, to yank them about and ride away from the danger. They were swearing and roaring and the tumult of thundering hoofs was rising, rising, rising in a great torrent of wrath in their wake.

'*Get back*!' bawled Hiller at the top of his voice as he tried to jockey his mount through the frenzy of terrified men and horses, now bunched together in a stumbling mass on the slope. '*Split up an' get the hell out of here, you damn' fools. Quit bunchin' up!*'

He was punishing his horse with big Spanish spurs and cursing the riders who continually jostled him or planted their animals in front of his in their own determined attempts to place as much distance as they could between themselves and that relentless storm of longhorns tearing along on their tails.

Dan Bryce, jogging madly in his saddle at the rear of the stampeding herd, was getting a measure of grim satisfaction out of seeing Pete Hiller and his gang in this predicament. Riding with Jim Phillimore, Charlie

Manders and others of the Muleshoe outfit, he fired his Colt into the air at spaced intervals. All along the line at the back of the running cattle, Muleshoe wranglers were doing the same thing with cold determination. Even Washington the Muleshoe cook had cut loose a horse from the *remuda* and was plunging along puncturing the dusty air with his old Smith & Wesson, inwardly thinking that this was better than rustling up pork and beans.

Dust, like the sombre smoke of an artillery onslaught, fogged the tawny slope. The slope was rapidly becoming a jostling torrent of upward sweeping longhorns, tearing along in a great fear-driven tide.

Up ahead, one of the rustlers yelled a final hoarse scream as the rushing tide caught him, jostled him from his saddle and swallowed him, and a second man went down under the swamping cattle with both arms held upwards like a drowning man.

And still the Muleshoe herd thundered on in its merciless rush in the wake of the panicking rustlers. There was a wild tangle of hastening rustlers high on the crest of the hump now, racing to get clear of the terror-on-the-hoof. Some broke clear and split the wind for the distant line of hills and rock needles. Others were less fortunate. Men who had joined up with Pete Hiller in his newly formed criminal outfit to butcher cowpokes and reap the benefits of theft were tossed from horses which could not outstrip the concentrated rush of cattle. They died beneath the herd.

Now, the beef swept down the far slope. Rustlers were hazing every which way and the thundering herd was losing its initial fury. The stampede was breaking up with knots of cattle running for the distance in confusion.

Dan Bryce, leading a party of Muleshoe men, shoved his game little bronc through the thinning cattle. He had kept the bulky figure of Pete Hiller in view through most of the charge and saw that the rustler leader was ahead, riding with a knot of his men in a bee-line for the hills. The black-clad man and his companions thrust their way through loping longhorns, came out of the ranks of the herd and rode in the wake of the hazing rustler chief and his men like dust-peppered demons.

They pressed hard and began to gain on them. Dan, knowing all that release of pent-up fury he had known in the past when mixing it with lawbreakers, bawled: 'Quit runnin' Hiller! You can't win! It's the law an' a long rope for you!'

Pete Hiller reacted to the challenging voice with a speedy and angry action. He jerked his mount to a halt in its tracks, slewed it around and faced the oncoming riders with a face as black as a thunder-cloud and with eyes smouldering in a crazy way. It was the face of a killer who knew he was licked — but who was going to kill again. Bryce, well to the fore of the onward plunging party of riders, saw that most of Hiller's companions were also turning their horses about.

Among them, he saw the face of Rufe Hogan, then that of Kid Billings. A surge of cold emotion swept through him and he knew that now he was going to fight out the final battle. It would embody vengeance for the night-herders killed on the night Criswell's hired guns scattered the gathered cattle before they left Llano Diablo; vengeance for the trampling of Mex Salinas, too. And there would be an element of a former fight in it as that part of his own personal past — the unfinished business of cleaning up Dutch Kloot's outfit — played its part in this battle.

For Kid Billings knew that he could not run this time. The kid was going to fight and Bryce could see that the young outlaw was out to kill him — *now* . . .

Gunfighter's savvy told Bryce what the kid was about to do a fleeting fraction of time before Billings, with his face screwed into a mask of hatred, threw the mouth of his Colt on Dan.

Bryce ducked in the saddle and fired with a brisk, fluid action in which he scarcely seemed to move at all.

Kid Billings went falling backwards out of his saddle like a wooden puppet.

Hiller and Hogan were held in a moment of surprise. For Bryce, only their faces were discernible against the tight knot of rustlers who turned their anonymous features to the Muleshoe men to make their last stand. A crackle of firing slashed between the two clashing factions of mounted men. There was a whinnying of horses, a yelling of stricken men and the deafening racket of exploding guns. But those two men were still alive and in their saddles: their faces contorted into vicious lines, their guns coming up to blast Dan Bryce out of saddle leather.

To Bryce, it seemed he was engaged in an isolated personal battle which was being acted out in the thick of the welter of the gunfight with unreal slowness. Maybe, he thought desperately, that bullet wound in his arm was worse than it seemed; maybe he was half delirious, maybe he was fevered and sick and weakened and maybe he was going to be gunned down in this, his last clash with the lawless ones.

He acted in a half dream, his bronc, scared by the too close exchange of slamming shots, was plunging almost upon Hiller's horse and Hiller was about to shoot . . .

Bryce's Colt coughed out a rope of fire which hit Pete Hiller in the chest and slammed him backwards, his pistol loosing a final protesting shot at the sky as he went. The din-torn world seemed to explode in one vivid flash as Rufe Hogan fired at Bryce, but the man from New Mexico was dropping across his saddle-horn, seeking the protection of the bronc's neck even as Hogan fired. He felt the scream of the bullet against his ear and knew the burning blast of muzzle-fire searing the flesh of his face and the Colt was bucking in his hand even before the flash of Hogan's gun had quite ceased to blind him. He had a ghostly vision of Hogan's doughy face, at close quarters, looking at him round-eyed and almost appealing. Then it was gone in a fog of smoke.

Bryce gripped his bronc with his knees to keep on the back of the crazily plunging animal. He shook his head like a wet terrier. He seemed to be lost in a night-black gloom of gunsmoke and there was an unreal silence. Someone grabbed him by the shoulder.

'You all right, Dan?' asked the voice of Charlie Manders.

Dan came back to reality. The shooting was over. What was left of the Hiller crew after the furious close-quarter battle was being rounded up by a strong party of Muleshoe cowboys. The rustlers, leaderless and licked hollow, had learned the better part of valour. They had thrown down their guns and were holding their hands up.

Jim Phillimore, his face and beard

powder blackened, was quickly beside Bryce.

'I thought them hellions was goin' to get you,' he shouted. 'I never saw anyone shoot so blamed fast as you did — it was lightnin'!'

'It seemed almighty slow to me,' Bryce confessed. 'I felt like I was goin' to faint for a minute. I think that nick in the arm made me lose more blood than I imagined. Any of our men hurt?'

'Two or three hurt, an' a couple dead,' Phillimore informed him, 'but, by grab, we got ourselves a rustler gang today. An' not just any old gang, it was Pete Hiller's crew. These galoots have had enough fightin', they're even goin' to show us where Criswell an' his wranglers an' herd are hidden!'

*　*　*

'I'm obliged to you, Phillimore,' said Jeff Criswell, shoving tobacco into his pipe. 'I'm mightily obliged to you.'

'You don't need to mention it,'

242

growled Big Jim Phillimore. 'We're neighbours, ain't we? I felt I had a duty to pull you out of this hole.'

They were squatting by the running water in the hidden valley, watching the Spur Barb cattle watering and grazing peacefully. Muleshoe wranglers and Spur Barb men were sharing smokes and coffee as they had done on the ranges during round-up times in other days.

There had been the briefest of battles as the skeleton force which Hiller had left in the valley had tried to defend their cattle and prisoners when the Muleshoe crew came roaring in. But it had soon petered out and the defenders were now securely-bound prisoners, along with the rest of Hiller's bunch, ready to be handed over when the law came in response to a summons which had been sent to the nearest settlement by a Muleshoe rider. A truce that looked like developing into a lasting peace was established between the two trail outfits.

'I've been a fool, Jim,' Criswell confessed. 'Acted plumb foolish over fencin' that disputed land, then built up a packet of trouble for myself by takin' on them gunhands. I admit I had your letters opened at the express office but there's one thing I want you to know: I didn't plant that feller in the rocks to shoot at Bryce. That was Hogan's idea. An' I didn't give any orders for your night-herders to be killed, that was Hogan again. He got a hell of a lot of power at Spur Barb — almost ran the place, thanks to my stupidity. I should have listened to Sid Clifford.'

Dan Bryce was nearby, rolling a smoke. 'How about that stampede the night of the storm?' he asked quietly.

Criswell hung his head. 'I admit I condoned that move an' I even agreed to Hogan's suggestion that he attempted to finish you off, Bryce. I don't know what I was thinkin' about. I was mad about the Mariposa Pass trick an' that Hogan *hombre* somehow worked on me like an evil influence. Jim will tell you

I'm no gentle Annie. He has cause to tell you I'm a plumb greedy grasper — but I'm no killer.' He looked appealingly at Phillimore.

'It's true,' confirmed Phillimore. 'I was never willin' to believe you'd turn to outright murder, whatever else you've done.'

Dan Bryce nodded, remembering the way he'd reflected on the point that Hogan was the true evil genius of the Spur Barb outfit.

'I guess the whole thing should be forgotten,' grinned Bryce.

'I guess it should,' agreed Phillimore. 'It would never have started if my boys hadn't been plumb bad-tempered about that fence an' fired at Criswell's boys.'

'They didn't do any harm. They were behavin' like a bunch of kids an' shootin' over each other's heads,' Criswell said. 'But I should have seen the danger signal an' hauled that fence down, 'stead of doin' what I did.'

'All right, all right!' bawled Phillimore. 'The hatchet is buried, Criswell

— we're neighbours again, at least we're as much neighbours as we'll ever be, you bad-tempered, scrawny little dried-out polecat!'

For the first time since anyone could remember Jeff Criswell was seen to grin with genuine good humour.

'All right. We're neighbours again,' he agreed. 'I'll gather up my herd an' take it out of the valley an' head right back home to tear up that blamed fence. The Dodge City contract is yours, Phillimore.'

Big Jim Phillimore tugged at his whiskers. Bryce noticed that in the last few hours he seemed to become bigger and more forceful; now, he looked exactly like the old Phillimore of years back.

'Now wait a minute. Criswell,' he bellowed. 'Allowin' there's been a few dirty tricks pulled, I admit I'm enjoyin' matchin' your crew in a race to Dodge. We'll continue it, by thunder. First outfit at the railhead gets the contract an' buys drinks for the losers when they get in. Agreed?'

'Agreed!' confirmed Criswell, extending his hand.

Dan Bryce, leaning against a tree, finishing his smoke, grinned at Charlie Manders.

'Looks like we're in for more hard ridin', Charlie,' he commented. He felt weary and the bullet-bite in his arm was giving sharp twinges of pain, but he grinned at the prospect of continuing the race to Dodge City.

It would be a clean fight and there would be great pleasure in taking part in it — as a hired cowhand and not a hired gun!

THE END

Other titles in the
Linford Western Library:

DIVIDED LOYALTIES

Ethan Flagg

Outlaw gang leader Curly Ben Clovis hears of shipments of silver stored at Hashknife in southern Colorado. He sends his lieutenant, Jim Kane, to suss out the best way of seizing the silver. When Kane is mistaken for the new lawman he assumes the guise of Marshal Jonas Kelly in order to secretly organize the robbery. But then he becomes embroiled in a dilemma where he is forced to make choices that will lead to double-dealing and bloodshed.

PATHS OF DEATH

P. McCormac

He had done with killing. That was all in the past. Zacchaeus Wolfe was a peaceful dirt farmer. But the Lazy K didn't like sodbusters. The Kerfoots owned the range . . . and the law. His little farm did not fit into their plans. So old man Barrett Kerfoot and his five sons, backed by a full complement of cowboys, began to push Zacchaeus. But they'd find out the hard way what it was to have a curly wolf by the tail . . .